The Alchemist

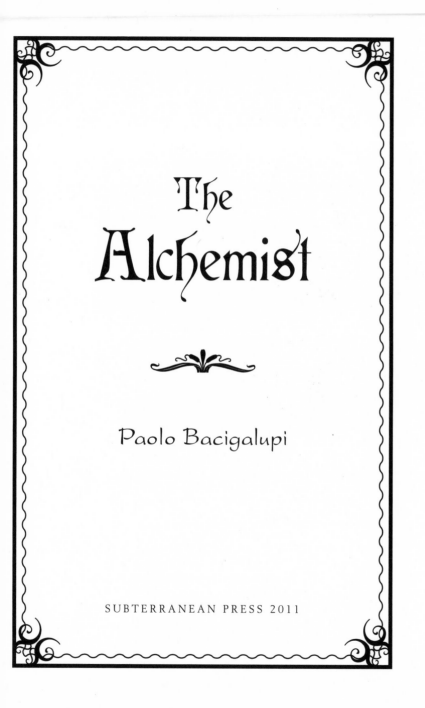

The
Alchemist

Paolo Bacigalupi

SUBTERRANEAN PRESS 2011

Subterranean Press
PO Box 190106
Burton, MI 48519

www.subterraneanpress.com

Introduction

by Tobias S. Buckell

I FIRST MET PAOLO AT a novel workshop called Blue Heaven. I eagerly had read the novel he was workshopping: *The Windup Girl*. I was bowled over by the depth of creation and thought that had gone into it, the evocative language, and the tortured characters. Here was the next William Gibson, I thought. The fact that Paolo also ended up being an insanely fun person to be around was just total icing.

We were using Skype to videochat every couple days while working on new novels. Just checking in with each other to see how we were doing. And during that time I started talking to Paolo about this novella I was trying to write in my spare time that was being commissioned by Audible. They wanted me to find a second writer, so that we could create a pair of related novellas.

I asked Paolo if he wanted to be the other author.

One thing writers are often wary of is getting stuck in a rut. As a result, I was excited to be writing a high fantasy novella, as I wrote mainly science fiction. Paolo also mainly wrote science fiction, so he was interested in trying something different. We both started to get excited about the idea.

The Alchemist, Paolo's story, grew out of the fact that Paolo was responsible for leading our two-person brain trust down many of the paths that built this unique world. While I had some notion about a creeping, living mass taking over the landscape, it was Paolo who wondered if it could be related to the use of magic: thus cementing the tales' respective focuses on consequences around the use of magic.

It was also the character of the Alchemist that led to us deciding to play with a Renaissance sort of feel for the stories, with brass, leather, glass and chemicals, and early firearms, all intermixed with tales of magic from the near-East. Before hardly any words had been written, I knew we had a unique canvas for our stories to play across.

And so herein lies a tale of the tragedy of good intentions, good inventions, love, family, unintended consequences, and magic and alchemy. It's a fantastic read, and it was just as fantastic seeing it come to life as Paolo wrote it. I hope you enjoy it as much as I did.

I

I T'S DIFFICULT TO SELL your last bed to a neighbor. More difficult still when your only child clings like a spider monkey to its frame, and screams as if you were chopping off her arms with an axe every time you try to remove her.

The four men from Alacan had already arrived, hungry and happy to make copper from the use of their muscles, and Lizca Sharma was there as well, her skirts glittering with diamond wealth, there to supervise the four-poster's removal and make sure it wasn't damaged in the transfer.

The bed was a massive piece of furniture. For a child, ridiculous. Jiala's small limbs had no need to sprawl across such a vast expanse. But the frame had been carved with images of the floating palaces of Jhandpara. Cloud dragons of old twined up its posts to the canopy where wooden claws clutched rolled nets and, with a clever copper clasp, opened on hinges to let the nets come tumbling down during the hot times to keep out mosquitoes. A beautiful bed. A fanciful bed. Imbued with the vitality of Jhandpara's lost glory. An antique made of kestrel-wood—that fine red grain so long choked under bramble—and triply valuable because of it.

We would eat for months on its sale.

But to Jiala, six years old and deeply attached, who had already watched every other piece of our household furniture disappear, it was another matter.

She had watched our servants and nannies evaporate as water droplets hiss to mist on a hot griddle. She had watched draperies tumble, seen the geometries of our carpets rolled and carried out on Alacaner backs, a train of men like linked sausages marching from our marbled halls. The bed was too much. These days, our halls echoed with only our few remaining footfalls. The porticos carried no sound of music from our pianoforte, and the last bit of warmth in the house could only be found in the sulphurous stink of my workshop, where a lone fire yet blazed.

For Jiala, the disappearance of her vast and beautiful bed was her last chance to make a stand.

"NOOOOOOOO!"

I tried to cajole her, and then to drag her. But she'd grown since her days as a babe, and desperation gave her strength. As I hauled her from the mattress, she grabbed hold of one huge post and locked her arms around it. She pressed her cheek against the cloud dragon's scales and screamed again. "NOOOOOOOO!"

We all covered our ears as she hit a new crystal-shattering octave.

"NOOOOOOOO!"

"Please, Jiala," I begged. "I'll buy you a new one. As soon as we have money."

"I don't want a new one!" she screamed. "I want this one!" Tears ran down her reddening face.

I tugged at her, embarrassed under the judging gaze of Mistress Lizca and the workmen behind me. I liked Lizca.

And now she saw me at my most reduced. As if the empty house wasn't enough. As if this sale of my child's last belonging was not humiliating in the extreme, I now begged a child for cooperation.

"Jiala. It's only for a little while. And it will just be down the narrows at Mistress Lizca's. You can visit if you like." I looked to Lizca, hoping desperately that she wouldn't contradict. "It will be just next door."

"I can't sleep next door! This is mine! You sold everything! We don't have anything! This is mine!" Jiala's shrieks rose to new levels, and this brought on her coughing, which alternated with her screams as I tried to pry her arms free.

"I'll buy you a new one," I said. "One fit for a princess."

But she only screamed louder.

The workmen kept their hands over their ears as the gryphon shrieks continued. I cast about, desperate for a solution to her heartbreak. Desperate to stop the coughing that she was inflicting on herself with this tantrum.

Stupid. I'd been stupid. I should have asked Pila to take her out, and then ordered the workmen to come stealthy like thieves. I cast about the room, and there on the workmen's faces, I saw something unexpected. Unlike Lizca, who stood stonily irritated, the workmen showed nothing of the sort.

No impatience.

No anger.

No superiority nor disgust.

Pity.

These refugee workmen, come across the river from Lesser Khaim to do a bit of labor for a few coppers, pitied me. Soiled linen shirts draped off their stooped shoulders and broken leather shoes showed cold mudcaked winter toes, and yet they pitied me.

They had lost everything fleeing their own city, their last portable belongings clanking on their backs, their hounds and children squalling and snot-nosed, tangled around their ankles. Flotsam in a river of refugees come from Alacan when their Mayor and Majisters accepted that the city could not be held and that they must, in fact, fall back—and quickly—if they wished to escape the bramble onslaught.

Alacan men, men who had lost everything, looked at me with pity. And it filled me with rage.

I shouted at Jiala. "Well, what should I do? Should I have you starve? Should I stop feeding you and Pila? Should we all sit in the straw and gnaw mice bones through the winter so that you can have a kestrel-wood bed?"

Of course, she only screamed louder. But now it was out of fear. And yet I continued to shout, my voice increasing, overwhelming hers, an animal roar, seeking to frighten and intimidate that which I could not cajole. Using my size and power to crush something small and desperate.

"Shut up!" I screamed. "We have nothing! Do you understand? Nothing! We have no choices left!"

Jiala collapsed into sobbing misery, which turned to deeper coughing, which frightened me even more, because if the coughing continued I would have to cast a spell to keep it down. Everything I did led only to something worse.

The fight went out of Jiala. I pried her away from the bed.

Lizca motioned to the Alacaners and they began the process of disassembling the great thing.

I held Jiala close, feeling her shaking and sobbing, still loud but without a fight now. I had broken her will. An ugly solution that reduced us both into something less than what the Three Faces of Mara hoped for us. Not father and daughter. Not protector and sacred charge. Monster and victim. I clutched my child to me, hating what had been conjured between us. That I had bullied her down. That she had forced me to this point.

But hating myself, most of all, for I had placed us in this position.

That was the true sickness. I had dragged us into danger and want. Our house had once been so very fine. In our glory days, when Merali was still alive, I made copper pots for rich households, designed metal and glass mirrors of exquisite inlay. Blew glass bargaining bulbs for the great mustached merchants of Diamond Street to drink from as they made their contracts. I engraved vases with the Three Faces of Mara: woman, man, and child, dancing. I etched designs of cloud dragons and floating palaces. I cast gryphons in gold and bronze and copper. I inlaid forest hunts of stags and unicorns in the towering kestrel forests of the East and sculpted representations of the three hundred and thirty-three arches of Jhandpara's glorious waterfront. I traded in the nostalgic dreams of empire's many lost wonders.

And we had been rich.

Now, instead of adornments for rich households, strange devices squatted and bubbled and clanked in my workroom, and not a single one of them for sale. Curving copper tubes twisted like kraken tentacles. Our impoverished faces reflected from the brass bells of delivery nozzles. Glass bulbs glowed blue with the ethereal stamens of the lora flower, which can only be gathered in summer twilight when ember beetles beckon them open and mate within their satin petals.

And now, all day and all night, my workroom hissed and steamed with the sulphurous residues of bramble.

Burned branches and seeds and sleep-inducing spines passed through my equipment's bowels. Instead of Jhandpara's many dreams, I worked now with its singular nightmare. The plant that had destroyed an empire and now threatened to destroy us as well. Our whole house stank day and night with the smell of burning bramble and the workings of my balanthast. That was the true cause of my daughter's pitched defense of her kestrel-wood bed.

I was the one at fault. Not the girl. I had impoverished us with every decision I had made, over fifteen years. Jiala was too young to even know what the household had looked like in its true glory days. She had arrived too late for that. Never saw its flowering rose gardens and lupine beds. Didn't remember when the halls rang with servants' laughter and activity, when Pila, Saema and Traz all lived with us, and Niaz and Romara and—some other servant whose name even I have now forgotten—swept every corner of the place for dust and kept the mice at bay. It was my fault.

I clutched my sobbing child to my breast, because I knew she was right, and I was wrong, but still I let Mistress Lizca and her Alacan workmen break the bed apart, and carry it out, piece by piece, until we were alone in an empty and cold marble room.

I had no choice. Or, more precisely, I had stripped us of our choices. I had gone too far, and circumstances were closing upon us both.

2

JIALA KEPT FROM ME for several days after I sold her bed. She went out, and disappeared for hours at a time. She was resentful, but she spoke no more to me, and seemed willing to let me bribe her back to forgiveness with syrup crackers from Sugar Alley. She disappeared into the cobbled streets of Khaim, and I took advantage of the peaceful time to work.

The sale of the bed, even if it was a fabulously rare piece of art, even if it did come from kestrel-wood which no one had been able to harvest in more than five decades as the bramble sprawl overwhelmed its cathedral forests, would only last so long. And after the money ran out, I would have no more options.

I felt as if I was trapped in the famous torture room of Majister Halizak, who liked to magic his victims into a closed cell, without door or window, and then slowly spell the whole room down from the size of an elephant to the size of a mouse. It was said that Halizak took great pleasure listening to people's screams. And then, as their prison shrank beyond their ability to bear, he would place a goblet below the tiny stone box, to catch the juices of his dying enemies and drink to his own long health.

But I was close.

Halizak's Prison was closing down on me. But unlike Halizak's victims, I now spied a door. A gap in my squeezing prison. We would not go without a home. Jiala and I would not be forced across the river to Lesser Khaim to live with the refugees of bramble spread.

I would be a hero. Recognized through the ages. I was going to be a hero.

Once again, I primed my balanthast.

Pila, my last faithful servant, watched from beside the fireplace. She had gone from a smiling young girl to a grown woman who now looked at me with a cocked head and a thoughtful expression as if I was already mad. She had brought in the final bits of my refashioned device, and my workshop was a new disaster of brass nails, armatures, and iron filings. The debris of inspiration.

I smiled at Pila. "This time it will work," I said.

The reek of burnt neem and mint filled the air. In the glass chamber atop the balanthast, a few sprigs of mint lay with bay and lora flower and the woody shavings of the neem.

I struck a match. Its flame gleamed. I was close. So very close. But Pila had seen other failures…

Pounding on the door interrupted my preparation.

I turned, annoyed. "Go answer," I told Pila. "Tell them I am busy."

I prepared again to ignite the balanthast, but premonition stayed my hand. Instead, I listened. A moment passed. And then a shriek echoed through the halls. Anguish and loss. I dropped the match and ran for the door.

Falzi the butcher stood at the threshold, cradling Jiala in his huge arms. She dangled limp, head lolling.

"I found her in a bramble," he said. "Deep in. I had to use a hook to pull her out, it was closing on her." Pila and I both reached for her, but Falzi pulled away from us. "You don't have the clothes for it." And indeed, his own leather shirt and apron were covered in pale thready bramble hairs. They fairly seemed to quiver with wormy malevolence. Even a few were dangerous, and Jiala's body was furred with them.

I stared, horrified. "But what was she doing there?" Jiala knew enough of bramble from my own work to avoid its beckoning vines. "She shouldn't have been anywhere near bramble."

"Street urchins…" Falzi looked away, embarrassed at the implication, but plunged on. "The Mayor offers a reward for bramble seeds collected in the city. To prevent the spread. A copper for a sack. Better pay than catching rats. Some children… if they are hungry enough, will go to the big brambles in the fields and burn it back. Then gather the seeds when the pods explode."

"My workshop," I said. "Quickly!"

Falzi carried Jiala's small body easily. Set her on the stones by the fire. "What will you do?" he asked. "The poison's already in her."

I shook my head as I used a brush to push away the bramble threads that clung to her. Redness stained her flesh wherever they touched. Poison and sleep, coursing beneath her skin. When I'd cleared a place on her throat, I pressed my fingers to her pulse, feeling for the echo of her heart.

Slow. So very slow.

"I have supplies that may help," I said. "Go. Thank you. But go!"

Falzi touched his heart in farewell. Shaking his head, he left us alone.

"Close the doors, Pila." I said. "And the windows."

"But—"

"Do it! And don't come within. Lock the doors."

WHEN I first thought that I might have a method of killing bramble, it was because I noticed how it never grew around the copper mines of Kesh. Even as Alacan fell and landholders retreated all along the line of bramble's encroach, the copper mines remained pristine.

Of course, over time it became impossible to get to the mines. Bramble surrounded that strange island of immunity and continued its long march west into Alacan. The delicate strand of road that led through the bramble forest to the copper mines became impossible to defend.

But the copper mines remained safe, long after everything else was swallowed. I noticed the phenomenon on my trips there to secure new materials for my business. Keshian copper made fine urns that were much in demand from my patrons and so I made the journey often. I remember making my careful way down that long bramble tunnel when workers still fought to keep the road to the mines open. Remember the worker's faces sooty and sweaty with the constant chopping and burning, their leather bladder sacks and brass-nozzled burners always alight and smoking as they spread flaming paste upon the poisonous plant.

And then the copper mines, opening before me. The deep holes and scrapings of mine work, but also grasslands and trees—the huge bramble growing all around its perimeter, but none inside. An oasis.

A few majisters and scholars also noticed the Keshian copper mines' unique qualities, but by the time anyone sought the cause of the place's survival, the bramble was coming strong, and soon no one could hack their way back to that isolated place of mining tools and tailings ponds for more investigation.

Of course, people experimented.

A few people thought to beat copper into our roads, or created copper knives to cut through the bramble, thinking that the metal was bramble's bane. And certainly some people even started to call it that. Copper charms sold well for a brief time. I admit that I even trafficked in such baubles, casting amulets and beating fine urns to ward off its encroach. But soon enough, people discovered that copper gave root to bramble as easily as a farmer's tilled field and the mortar of Alacan's massive city walls. Granite was better at warding off the plant, but even that gave root eventually.

Even so, the Keshian copper mines remained in my mind, much as they likely remained in the deep bramble forest, a dream of survival, if only we could puzzle it out. And so now, from memory, I sought to reconstruct the conditions of Kesh in the environs of my workshop, experimenting with the natural interactions of flora and ore, seeking that singular formula which had stalled bramble in its march.

THE DOOR closed behind Pila. I felt again for Jiala's pulse. It was nearly gone. The drug of bramble has been used by assassins and thwarted lovers. Its poison produces an overwhelming sleep that succumbs to deeper darkness. It squeezes the heart and slows it until blood flows like cold syrup, and then stops entirely, frozen, preserving a body, sometimes for years, until rats and mice and flies burrow deep and tear the body apart from within.

And now bramble's poisonous threads covered Jiala's skin. I took a copper rod and ran it over her arms. Then touched mint to her flesh. With a pair of brass pincers, I began plucking the threads from her skin. Setting them in a pottery bowl beside me so that I wouldn't carelessly touch them myself. Working as quickly as I could. Knowing that I couldn't work fast enough. There were dozens of them, dozens and dozens. More coated her clothing but they didn't matter. Her skin was covered. Too many, and yet still I plucked.

Jiala's eyelids fluttered. She gazed up from under heavy lashes, dark eyes thick with bramble's influence.

"Do I have enough?" she murmured.

"Enough what, child?" I continued plucking threads from her skin.

"Enough… seeds… to buy back my bed."

I tried to answer, but no words came. My heart felt as if it was squeezed by Halizak's Prison, running out liquid and dead.

Jiala's eyes closed, falling into the eternal sleep. I frantically felt after her heart's echo. A slow thud against my fingertip, sugar syrup running colder. Another thud. Thicker. Colder. The sluggish call of her heart. A longer pause, then…

Nothing.

I stumbled away from my dying girl, sick with my failures.

My balanthast lay before me, all its parts bubbling and prepared. In desperation, I seized it and dragged it over to my dying

daughter. I aimed its great brass bell at her inert form. Tears blurred my vision. I swept up a match, and then... paused.

I don't know why it came to me. It's said that the Three Faces of Mara come to us and whisper wisdom to us in our hour of need. That inspiration comes from true desperation and that the mysteries of the world can be so revealed. Certainly, Mara is the seed of life and hope.

I knelt beside Jiala and plucked a strand of hair from her head, a binding, a wish, a... I did not know, but suddenly I was desperate to have something of hers within the workings of the balanthast, and the bramble, too. All with the neem and mint... I placed her hair in the combustion chamber, and struck the match. Flame rose into the combustion chamber, burning neem and mint and bramble and Jiala's black hair, smoking, blazing, now one in their burn. I prayed to Mara's Three Faces for some mercy, and then twisted the balanthast's dial. The balanthast sucked the burning embers of her hair and the writhing threads of bramble and all the other ingredients into its belly chamber.

For a moment, nothing happened. Then blue flame exploded from the bell, enveloping Jiala.

WAKE UP, *papa.*
Wake up.
Wake.
Up.

Dim echoing words, pokes and proddings.

Wake up, Papa.
Papa?
Papa papa papapapapapa.

I opened my eyes.

Jiala knelt over me, a haziness of black hair and skinny brown limbs and blue skirts. Blurred and ethereal. Limned in an uncertain focus as light bound around her. A spirit creature from within the Halls of Judgment. Waiting for Borzai the Judge to gather her into his six arms, peer into her soul, and then pass her on to the Hall of Children, where innocents live under the protective gaze of dog-headed Kemaz.

I tried to sit up, couldn't. Lay back. The spirit creature remained, tugging at me. The workshop was a shambles, all of it blurry and unsteady, as if it lay on the plane of clouds.

All of us dead, then.

"*Papa?*"

I turned to her echoing voice. Stared at her. Stared again at the ravaged workroom. Something cold and sharp was pressing against my back. Not spirit-like at all.

Slowly, I dragged myself upright, leaning against the stone wall. I was lying far across the room from the fireplace. The balanthast lay beside me, its glass chambers shattered, its vacuum bulbs nothing but jagged teeth in their soldered sockets. Bent copper tubes gleamed all around me, like flower petals scattered to Mara during the planting march.

"Are you alright, Papa?" Jiala stared at me with great concern. "Your head is bloody."

I reached up and touched her small worried face. Warm. Alive. Not a spirit creature.

Whole and alive, her skin smoking with the yellow residue of bramble's ignition. Blackened threads of bramble ash covered her, her hair half-melted, writhing with bramble thread's death throes still. Singed and scalded and blistery but whole and miraculously alive.

I ran my hand down her scorched cheek, wonder-struck.

"Papa?"

"I'm alright, Jiala," I started to laugh. "More than alright."

I clutched her to me and sobbed. Thanking Mara for my daughter's salvation. Grateful for this suspended execution of my soul.

And beyond it, another thought, a wider hope. That bramble, for the first time in all my experiments, had truly died, leaving not even its last residue of poison behind.

Fifteen years is not too long to seek a means to save the world.

OF COURSE, NOTHING IS as simple as we
would wish.

After that first wild success, I succeeded in
producing a spectacular string of failures which culminated
in nearly exploding the house. More worrying to me, even
though Jiala survived her encounter with the bramble, her
cough was much worsened by it. The winter damp spurred
it on, and now she hacked and coughed daily, her small lungs
seemingly intent on closing down upon her.

She was too young to know how bad the cough had
been before—how much it had greatly concerned me. But
after the bramble, blood began staining her lips, the rouge
of her lungs brought forth by the evils that bramble had
worked upon her body as it sought to drive her down into
permanent sleep.

I avoided using magic for as long as possible, but Jiala's
cough worsened, digging deeper into her lungs. And it was
only a small magic. Just enough spelling to keep her alive.
To close the rents in her little lungs, and stop the blood from
spackling her lips. Perhaps a sprig of bramble would sprout
in some farmer's field as a result, fertilized by the power

released into the air, but really it was such a small magic, and Jiala's need was too great to ignore.

The chill of winter was always the worst. Khaim isn't like the northern lands, where freezes kill every living plant except bramble and lay snow over the ground in cold drifts and wind-sculpted ice. But still, the cold ate at her. And so, I took a little time away from my alchemy and the perfecting of the balanthast to work something within her.

Our secret.

Even Pila didn't know. No one could be allowed to know but us.

Jiala and I sat in the corner of my workshop, amidst the blankets where she now slept near the fire, the only warm room I had left, and I used the scribbled notes from the book of Majister Arun to make magic.

His pen was clear, even if he was long gone to the Executioner's axe. His ideas on vellum. His hand reaching across time. His past carrying into our future through the wonders of ink. Rosemary and pkana flower and licorice root, and the deep soothing cream of goat's milk. Powdered together, the yellow pkana flower's petals all crackling like fire as they touched the milk. Sending up a smoke of dreams.

And then with my ring finger, long missing all three gold rings of marriage, I touched the paste to Jiala's forehead, between the thick dark hairs of her eyebrows. And then, pulling down her blouse, another at her sternum, at the center of her lungs. The pkana's yellow mark pulsed on her skin, seeming wont to ignite.

As we worked this little magic, I imagined the great majisters of Jhandpara healing crowds from their arched balconies.

It was said that people came for miles to be healed. They used the stuff of magic wildly, then.

"Papa, you mustn't." Jiala whispered. Another cough caught her, jerking her forward and reaching deep, squeezing her lungs as the strongman squeezes a pomegranate to watch red blood run between his fingers.

"Of course I must," I answered. "Now be quiet."

"They will catch you, though. The smell of it—"

"Shhhh."

And then I read the ancient words of Majister Arun, sounding out the language that could never be recalled after it was spoken. Consonants burned my tongue as it tapped those words of power. The power of ancients. The dream of Jhandpara.

The sulphur smell of magic filled the room, and now round vowels of healing tumbled from my lips, spinning like pin wheels, finding their targets in the yellow paste of my fingerprints.

The magic burrowed into Jiala, and then it was gone. The pkana flower paste took on a greenish tinge as it was used up, and the room filled completely with the smoke of power unleashed. Astonishing power, all around, and only a little effort and a few words to bind it to us. Magic. The power to do anything. Destroy an empire, even.

I cracked open the shutters, and peered out onto the black cobbled streets. No one was outside, and I fanned the room quickly, clearing the stench of magic.

"Papa. What if they catch you?"

"They won't." I smiled. "This is a small magic. Not some great bridge-building project. Not even a spell of fertility. Your lungs hold small wounds. No one will ever know. And

I will perfect the balanthast soon. And then no one will ever have to hold back with these small magics ever again. All will be well."

"They say that the Executioner sometimes swings wild, doesn't chop a man in half with kindness. But makes him flop instead. That the Mayor pays him extra to make an example of the people who use magic."

"It's not true."

"I saw one."

"No, you didn't."

"It was last week. At the gold market. Right in the square. I was with Pila. And the crowd was so thick we couldn't leave. And Pila covered my eyes, but I could see through her fingers. And the Executioner chopped and chopped and chopped and chopped and the man yelled so loud and then he stopped, but still he didn't do a good job. Not a clean cut at all, the pig lady said. Said she does better with her swine."

I made myself smile. "Well, that's not our problem. Everyone does a little magic. No one will mind us. As long as we don't rub anyone's nose in it."

"I wouldn't want to see you chopped and chopped and chopped."

"Then make sure you drink Pila's licorice tea and stay out of the cold. It's a hard thing to keep secrets. But secrets are best when there are only two to know." I touched her forehead. "You and I."

I pulled my mustaches. "Tug for luck?"

But she wouldn't. And she wasn't consoled.

A MONTH later, as the muddy rags of cruel spring snow turned to the sweet stink of wet warming earth, I made the last adjustments to the balanthast and set it loose on the bramble wall.

We left the city deep in the night, making our way east over muddy roads, the balanthast bundled on my back. Jiala, Pila and I. With the embrace of darkness, the women of the bramble crews with their fire and hatchets were gone, and the children who gathered seeds behind them in careful lines had given up. There would be no witnesses to our experiment. The night was chill and uncomfortable. We held our torches high.

It took only two hours to reach the bramble wall, much to my surprise.

"It's moved," I muttered.

Pila nodded. "The women who sell potatoes say they've lost more fields. Some of them before they had a chance to dig up the last of their crop."

The bramble loomed above us, many tangled layers, the leading edge of an impenetrable forest that stretched all the way to fabled Jhandpara. In the light of the torches the bramble threw off strange hungry shadows, seeming eager to tug us into its sleep-inducing embrace. I thrust my torch amongst its serpent vines. Tendrils crackled and curled in the heat, and a few seed pods, fat as milkweed, burst open, spilling new seeds onto the ground.

Tender green growths showed all along the edge where the bramble crews had been burning and pruning, but deep within, the bramble had turned woody, impenetrable, and thick. Sharp blood-letting thorns glinted in the torchlight, but more troublesome were the pale fine hairs shimmering everywhere, coating every vine's length, the venomous fibers that Jiala had so nearly succumbed to.

I took a breath, unnerved despite myself in the presence of our implacable enemy.

"Well," Pila said. "You wanted to show us."

My faith faltered. Small experiments in the workshop were one thing. But out in the open? Before my daughter and Pila? I cursed myself for my pride. I should have come to test the balanthast in private. Not like this where all my failures could be mocked or pitied.

"Well?" Pila said.

"Yes," I said. "Yes. We'll get started."

But still I delayed.

Pila gave me a look of disgust and started setting out the kestrel-wood tripod. She had grown insolent over the years, as her salary had been reduced and her responsibilities increased. Not at all the young shy girl she had been when she first came to the house. She now carried too much authority, and too much of a skeptical eye. Sometimes I suspected that I would have given up long ago on my experimentations, if not for Pila watching me with her silent judgments. It's easy to fail yourself, but failing before another, one who has watched you wager so much and so mightily on an uncertain future—well, that is too much shame to bear.

"Right," I murmured. "Of course."

I unbound the balanthast from my back. Set it upon the kestrel-wood to brace it. Since my first wild success, I had managed to dampen much of the balanthast's explosive reaction, venting it from rows of newly designed chimneys that puffed like a cloud dragon's nostrils. The balanthast now held fast and didn't topple and didn't blow one across the room to leave a body lying bruised and dazed. I crouched and made sure that the tripod was well set in the muddy earth.

To be honest, the tripod could have been made of anything, certainly something less extravagant. But kestrel-wood I loved. So hard and strong that even fire couldn't take it. The northmen of Czandia used to forge swords of kestrel-wood. Lighter than steel. Just as strong. The tripod seemed to say to me that we still had a future, that we might once again stand strong, and grow the wonders of old.

Or, if you were Pila, you called it the expensive affectation of a foolish man, even as she helped me fashion its sturdy base.

I straightened and unlimbered the rest of the balanthast's components. Pila and Jiala helped me assemble its many pieces.

"No," I whispered, and then realized that I was doing so and cleared my throat. "Jiala, put the vacuum chamber so that it faces forward, toward the mouth. And please be careful. I don't have enough fire to blow another."

"I'm always careful, Papa."

At last we were ready, the brass belly chamber and curling copper tubes and glass bulbs gleamed in the silver of the moon, a strange and unearthly thing.

"It looks like something that would have come out of Jhandpara," Pila said. "So much fine artistry, put into this one object."

I primed the combustion bulb of the balanthast. Neem and bay, and mint and twilight lora flower and a bramble clipping. By torchlight, we dug into the earth, seeking the root bundle. There were many. With leather-gloved hands, I scooped out a bit of earth, bramble's vessel. Mara's fertile womb. The necessary ingredient that would contain the alchemical reaction and channel it into the deeply embedded bramble, much as Jiala's hair had bound the reaction deep into her body. Saltpeter and sulphur and charcoal to drive the concoction home, poured into the belly chamber. I slid closed the combustion bulb, twisted the brass latches tight.

With a target now chosen, I thrust the balanthast's three newly-constructed nozzles into the earth beside it. Jiala covered her mouth with a tiny hand as I lit the match. I almost smiled. I set the match under the combustion bulb, and the assembled ingredients caught fire. It glowed like a firefly in its glassine chamber. Slowly the flame died. We watched. Breaths held.

And then as if the Three Faces of Mara had inhaled all at once, the entire careful wad disappeared, sucked into the belly chamber. The primed balanthast quivered with power, elements coming together.

The reaction was so sudden that we had no chance to brace. The very earth tossed us from our feet. Yellow acrid smoke billowed over us. A desperate animal shriek filled the air, as if the swine women were amongst the pigs in a sty, wounding and bleeding a great herd and not killing a single one. We gained our feet and ran, coughing and tearing, stumbling over muddy furrows. Jiala was worst taken. Her cough ripped deep into her lungs, making me fear I'd need to use the healing magic on her again before the night was over.

Slowly the smoke dispersed, revealing our work. The balanthast quivered on its tripod, steady still where it had been jammed into the earth, but now, all around it, there was a seething mass of bramble tendrils, all writhing and smoking. The vines hissed and burned, flakes of ash falling like scales from a dragon. Another shudder ran through the earth as deep roots writhed and ripped upward—and then, all at once, the vines collapsed, falling all to soot, leaving clear earth behind.

We approached cautiously. The balanthast had not only killed the root I had chosen, but destroyed horse-lengths of bramble in every direction. It would have taken workers hours to clear so much. I held up my torch, staring. Even at the perimeter of the balanthast's destruction, the bramble growth hung limp like rags. I stepped forward, cautious. Struck a damaged plant with a gloved hand. Its vines sizzled with escaping sap, and collapsed.

I swung about, staring at the ground. "Do you see any seeds?"

We swept our torches over the earth, straining to make out any of the pods which should have sprung out and burst open in the blaze of fire's heat.

Jiala squatted in the cold damp earth, turning it over and running it through her little gloved fingers.

"Well? Is there anything?"

Jiala looked up, amazed. "No, Papa."

"Pila?" I whispered. "Do you see any?"

"No." Astonishment marked her voice. "There are none. Not a single one."

Together, we continued our hunt. Nothing. Not a single seed disbursed from a single pod. The bramble vine had died, and left nothing of itself behind to torment us another day.

"It's magic," Pila whispered. "True magic."

I laughed at that. "Better than magic. Alchemy!"

THE NEXT MORNING, DESPITE the previous late night, we all woke with the first crowing of roosters. I laughed to find Pila and Jiala already clustered in the workroom, peering out the shutters, waiting for enough sunlight to see the final result.

As soon as the sun cracked the horizon, we were out in the fields again, headed across the muddy furrows to the bramble wall. The first of the bramble crews were already at work, with axes and long chopping knives, wearing leather aprons to protect themselves from the sleeping spines. Smoke from bramble's burn rose into the air, coiling snakes, black and oily. Dirty children walked in careful lines through the fields with shovels and hoes, uprooting new incursions. In the dawn light, with the levee labor all at the wall, it looked like the scene of some recent battle. The smoke, the hopeless faces. But as we approached the site of my balanthast firing, a small knot of workers huddled.

We slipped close.

"Have you come to see it?" they asked.

"See what?" Pila asked.

"There's a hole in the bramble." A woman pointed. "Look how deep it goes."

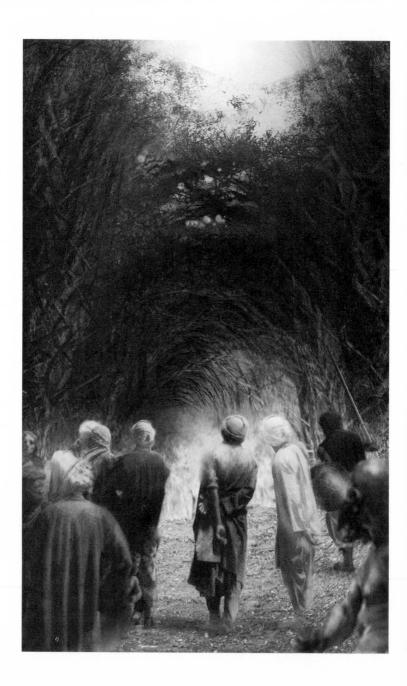

Several children squatted in the earth. One of them looked up. "It's clean, Mama. No seeds at all. It's like the bramble never came at all."

I could barely restrain my glee. Pila had to drag me away to keep me from blurting out my part. We rushed back to Khaim, laughing and skipping the whole way.

Back in our home, Pila and Jiala brought out my best clothes. Pila helped me work the double buttons of my finest vest, pursing her lips at the sight of how skinny I had become since I last wore the thing in my wealth and health.

I laughed at her concern.

"Soon I'll be fat again, and you'll have your own servants and we'll be rich and the city will saved."

Pila smiled. Her face had lost its worry for the first time in years. She looked young again, and I was struck with the memory of how fine she had been in youth, and how now, despite worry and years, she still stood, unbent and unbroken by the many responsibilities she had taken on. She had stuck with our household, even as our means had faltered, even as other, richer families offered a better, more comfortable life.

"It's very good that you are not mad, after all," Pila said.

I laughed. "You're very sure I'm not mad?"

She shrugged. "Well, not about bramble, at least."

THE WAY to Mayors House must pass around Malvia Hill, through the clay market and then down along the River Sulong, which splits Khaim from Lesser Khaim.

Along the river, the spice market runs into the potato market runs into the copper market. Powdered spices choke the air, along with the calls of spice men with their long black mustaches that they oil and stretch with every child. Their hands are red with chilies and yellow with turmeric, and their lungs give off the scents of clove and oregano. They sit under their archways along the river, with their big hemp bags of spice out front, and the doorways to their storehouses behind, where piled spices reach two stories high. And then on to the women in the potato market, where they used to sell only potatoes, but now sell any number of tubers, and then the copper families, who can beat out a pot or a tube, who fashion brass candlesticks for the rich and cooking pots for the poor.

When I was young, there was only Khaim. At that time, there was still a bit of the old Empire left. The great wonders of the East, and the great capital of Jhandpara were gone, but still, there was Alacan and Turis and Mimastiva. At that time, Khaim was a lesser seat, valued for its place on the river, but still, a far reach from Jhandpara where great majisters had once wielded their power and wore triple diamonds on their sleeves. But with the slow encroachment of the bramble, Khaim grew. And, across from it, Lesser Khaim grew even faster.

When I was a child, I could look across the river and see nothing but lemon trees and casro bushes, heavy with their dense fruits. Now refugees squatted and built mud huts there. Alacaners, who had destroyed their own homes and now insisted on destroying Khaim as well. Turis, of course is nothing but ash. But that wasn't their fault. Raiders took Turis, but Alacaners had only themselves to blame.

Jiala hurried along the river with me, her hand in mine. Small. So small. But now with a future. Not just a chance at life and wealth, but a chance that she would not run like the Alacaners from her home as bramble swallowed her childhood and history.

Out on the Sulong, tiny boats made their way back and forth across the water, carrying workers from Lesser Khaim into the main city. But now, something else marred the vista.

A great bridge hung in the air, partially constructed. It floated there, held down by ropes so that it would not fly free. Magic. Astonishing and powerful magic coming into play. The work of Majister Scacz, the one man in the city who wielded magic with the sanction of the Mayor, and so would never fear the Executioner's axe.

I paused, staring across the water to the floating bridge. Magic such as had not been seen since Jhandpara fell. Seeing it there, rising, it filled me with a superstitious dread. So much magic in one place. Even the balanthast couldn't protect against that much magic.

A spice man called out to me. "You want to buy? Or are you going to block my trade?"

I tipped my velvet hat to him. "So sorry, merchantman. I was looking at the bridge."

The man spat. Eyed the floating construction. "Lot of magic, there." He spat again. Tobacco and kehm root together. Narcotic. "I hear they're already chopping bramble on the far bank. Hardly any bramble on the west side at all, and now it's growing in the wagon ruts. Next thing, we'll be like Alacan. Swallowed by bramble because our jolly Mayor wants to connect here with there. Bad enough that all these new Alacaners use their small magics. Now we have big magic too. Scacz and the Mayor pretending Khaim should be another Jhandpara with majisters and diamonds and floating castles."

He spat more kehm root and tobacco, and eyed the bridge. "Executioner will be busy now. Sure as bramble creep, we'll have new heads spiked on city gates. Too much big magic to let the little magics run wild."

"Maybe not," I started, but Jiala pinched my hand and I fell silent.

The spice man eyed me as if I was mad. "I had to burn an entire sack of cloves, today. Whole sack I couldn't sell. Full of bramble seeds and sprout. Someone makes his little magic, ruins my business."

I wanted to tell him that the bundle on my back would change the balance, but Jiala, at least, had sense, and so I kept my words to myself. Magic brings bramble. A project like the bridge had an inevitable cost.

I hefted my bag of implements and we carried on, around the edge of the hill and then up its face to where Mayor's House looked down over Khaim.

WE WERE ushered into the Mayor's gallery without fuss. Marble floors and arches stretched around us. My clothes felt poor, Jiala's as well. Even our best was now old and worn.

In the sudden cool of the gallery, her cough started. A dry hacking thing that threatened to build. I knelt and gave her a sip of water. "Are you well?"

"Yes, Papa." She watched me, solemn and trusting. "I won't cough." And then immediately her dry cough started again. It echoed about, announcing our presence to all the other petitioners.

We sat in the gallery, waiting with the women who wanted to change their household tax and the men who were petitioning to escape levee labor. After an hour, the Mayor's secretary came to us, his medallion of office gleaming gold on his chest, the Axe of the Executioner crossed over the Staff of the Majister, the twin powers that the Mayor wielded for the benefit of the city. The secretary led us across another marble gallery, and thence into the Mayor's offices, and the door was shut behind us.

The Mayor wore red velvet and his own much larger medallion on a chain of gold around his neck. His fingers touched the medallion every so often, a needy gesture. And with him, the Majister Scacz. My skin prickled at the sight of one who used magic as a daily habit, passing the consequences of his activities onto the bramble crews and the children of the city who dug and burned the minor bits of bramble from between mortar stones and cobbles.

"Yes?" the Mayor asked. "You're who, then?"

"Jeoz, the alchemist," the secretary announced.

"And he reeks of magic," Majister Scacz murmured.

I made myself smile. "It is my device."

The Mayor's eyebrows rose, fuzzy gray caterpillars arching over his ruddy face. His mustache was short, no child in his history at all. An old scar puckered one side of his cheek, pulling his mouth into a slight smile. "You practice magic?" he asked sharply. "Are you mad?"

I made a placating gesture. "I do not practice, Excellency. No. Not at all." A nervous laugh escaped my lips. "I practice alchemy. It does not bring bramble. I have no dealings with the curse of Jhandpara." It was unbelievable how nervous I had become. "No need for the Executioner, here. None at all." I untied my bag and began pulling out the pieces of the balanthast. "You see…" I screwed one of the copper ends into its main chamber. Unwrapped the combustion bulb, breathing a sigh of relief that it had survived the trip. "You see," I repeated myself, "I have created something, which your Excellency will appreciate. I think."

Beside me, Jiala coughed. Whether from sickness, or nervousness, I couldn't say. Scacz's eyes went to her. Held. I didn't like the way he stared at her. His thoughtful expression. I plunged on.

"It is a balanthast."

The Mayor examined the device. "It looks more like an arquebus."

I made myself smile. "Not at all. Though it does use the reactants of fire. But my device has properties most extraordinary." My hands were shaking. I found the mint. The neem bark. Lora flower. Set them in the chamber.

Scacz was watching closely. "Am I watching sorcery, sir. Right before myself? Unsanctioned?"

"N-no." I shook under his examination. Tried to load the balanthast.

Jiala took it away. "Here, Papa."

"Y-yes. Good. Thank you, child." I took a deep breath. "You see, a balanthast destroys bramble. And not just a little. The balanthast reaches for a bramble's root and poisons it utterly. Place it within a yard or two of a heart root, and it will destroy more than a bramble crew can destroy in half a day."

The Mayor leaned close. "You have proof of this?"

"Yes. Of course. I'm sorry." I pulled a small clay pot shrouded in burlap out of my bag and put on my leather gloves before unwrapping it.

"Bramble," I explained.

They both sucked in their breath at the sight of the potted plant. I looked up at their consternation. "We use gloves."

"You carry bramble into the city?" the Mayor asked. "Deliberately?"

I hesitated. Finally I said, "It was necessary. For the testing. The science of alchemy requires much trial and error." Their faces were heavy with disapproval. I lit my match, and touched it to the glass bulb. Clamped it closed.

"Hold your breath, Jiala." I looked apologetically at the Mayor. "The smoke is quite acrid."

Mayor and Majister also sucked in their breaths. The balanthast shivered as its energy discharged. A ripple of death passed into the soil. The pot cracked as the bramble writhed and died.

"Magic!" Scacz cried, lunging forward. "What magic is this?"

"No, Majister! Alchemy. Magic has never been able to affect bramble. It does not sap bramble's poison, nor kill its seeds, nor burn back its branches. This is something new."

Scacz grabbed for the balanthast. "I must see this."

"It's not magic." I yanked the balanthast back, afraid that in his hurry he would destroy it. "It uses the natural properties of the neem," I said. "A special species, loved by majisters, yes, but this is merely the application of nature's principles. We vaporize the neem with a few other ingredients, force it through the tube, and with the aid of sulphur and saltpeter and charcoal, we send its essence into the earth. Even a small application does wonders. The neem essence binds with the root of the bramble. Kills it, as you see. Attracted like a fly to honey."

"And what causes neem to seek bramble?"

I shrugged. "It's difficult to say. Perhaps some magical residue or aura from the plant. I tried thousands of substances before the neem. Only the neem bark works so well."

"The neem is attracted to magic, you think?"

"Well," I hedged. "It is certainly attracted to bramble. Oil and water never mix. Neem and bramble seem the opposite. What causes the affinity..." I could feel myself starting to sweat under their combined gazes, not liking how Scacz obsessed with magic. "I hesitate to say that it's magic the neem essence finds so attractive..."

"You talk all around the root of the issue." Scacz said. "Worse than a priestess of Ruiz."

"Forgive me," I stammered. "I don't want you to think that I've been unwary in my investigations."

"He's worried we're about to send him off to the Executioner," the Mayor said.

I gave the man a sickly smile. "Quite. Bramble is unique. It has qualities that we may think of as magical—its astonishing growth, its resilience, the way that magic seems to fertilize its flourishing—but who can say what unique aspect causes the neem's essence to bind with it? These questions are beyond me. I experiment, I record my results, and I experiment again.

"The alchemical response to neem is bramble death. What causes that reaction, whether it is some magical residue that leeches from the bramble root and somehow makes it vulnerable to neem, or some other quality, I can't say. But it works. And works well. There is a plot of earth that I myself have cleared into the bramble wall. In the time it takes you to clap your hands three times, I cleared more land than this office occupies."

Mayor and Majister both straightened at the news.

"So quickly?" the Mayor asked.

I nodded vigorously. "Even today, it still shows no sign of regrowth. No seeds, you understand? Not a single one. With my device, you can arm the people and take back farmland. Push back the bramble wall. Save Khaim."

"Extraordinary," Scacz said. "Not just push the bramble back. Perhaps even reclaim the heart of the empire. Return to Jhandpara."

"Exactly." I couldn't help feeling relief as their expressions lost their skepticism.

The Mayor had begun to smile widely. He stood. "By the Three Faces of Mara, man, you've done something special!"

He motioned for Jiala and me. "Come! The two of you must have a glass of wine. This discovery is worth celebrating."

He laughed and joked with us as he guided us to a room with great windows that looked out over the city. Khaim jumbled down the hill below us. On the horizon, the sun was slowly sinking. Red sunlight filtered through the smoke and cookfires of lesser Khaim. The half-constructed floating bridge arched across the river like a leaping cat, held in place by great hemp ropes to keep it from sailing away as they worked to extend its skeleton.

"This couldn't come at a better time," the Mayor said. "Look out there, alchemist. Lesser Khaim grows every day. And not just from the refugees of Turis and Alacan. Others too, small holders who have been overwhelmed by the bramble. And they bring their magics with them.

"Before they came, we were nearly in balance. We could still cut back enough bramble to offset the bits of magic use. Even the bridge would have been acceptable. But the Alacaners are profligate with their magic, and now the bramble comes hard upon us. Their habits are crushing us. Everyone has some little magic that he or she believes is justified. And then when a bit of bramble roots in a neighbor's roof beams, who can say who caused it?"

He turned to me. "You know they call me the Jolly Mayor over there? Make fun of me for my scar and my poor humor." He scowled. "Of course I'm in a poor humor. We fight bramble every day, and every day it defeats us. If this keeps on, we'll be run out of here in three sixes of years."

I startled at his words. "Surely it's not that bad."

The Mayor raised his caterpillar brows. "Oh yes." He nodded at Jiala. "Your girl will be part of a river of refugees twice the size of the one we took in from Alacan." He turned again to look west. "And where will they go then? Mpaias? Loz? Turis is gone to raiders." He scowled. "Lesser Khaim is just as vulnerable. We barely fought off the raiders' last attack. Without the bridge, I cannot have a hope of defending that side of the river. And so we spend magic where we would prefer not to, and add to the problem. We're caught in Halizak's Prison, for certain."

His steward arrived with wine and goblets. I looked at the stemmed glasses with curiosity, wondering if I myself had long ago blown their shapes, but then recognized the distinctive mark of Saara Solso. She had improved since I used to compete with her. Another reminder of how long I had been at my project.

The steward paused on the verge of uncorking the wine bottle. "Are you certain about this, Excellency?" he asked.

The Mayor laughed and pointed at me. "This man comes to us with salvation, and you worry about an old vintage?"

The steward looked doubtful, but he uncorked the bottle anyway. A joyful scent filled the room. The Mayor looked at me, eyes twinkling. "You recognize it?" he asked. "The happy bouquet of history."

I was drawn by the scent, like a child to syrup crackers. Astonished and intoxicated, wide-eyed. "What is it?"

"Wine from the hillsides of Mount Sena, the summer vine-yards of the old empire," Majister Scacz said. "A rare thing, now that those hillsides are covered with bramble. Perhaps a score of bottles still exist, of which our Jolly Mayor possesses, now, two."

"Don't call me that."

Scacz bowed. "The name suits you today, Excellency."

The Mayor smiled. "For once."

The steward poured the wine into the glassine bulbs.

"Currant and cinnamon and joy." Majister Scacz was watching me. "You're about to taste one of the finest plea-sures of the Empire. Served at spring planting, for harvest and for flowering-age ceremonies. The richest merchants had fountains of it in their floating castles, if you can credit such a thing. Magic, make no mistake. The vintner's genius bound with the majister's craft."

He caught Jiala watching, her eyes shining at the scent. "Come, girl. Taste our lost history." He poured a splash into glass. "Not too much. You're too small to do more than taste, but I promise you, you will not forget this thing."

The Mayor held up his glass, ruby and black in the setting sun. "A toast, then, gentlemen. To our future, refound."

We drank, and the blood of the old empire coursed through our veins and made us giddy. We examined my instrument again, with the Majister and the Mayor making exclamations at the workmanship, at my methods for joining glass to copper, of metallurgy that had yielded a combustion chamber that would not crack with the power of the flames released. We talked of the difficulties of making more balanthasts and speculated how many miles we might clear of the surrounding countryside.

"It takes a great deal of trouble to make one," Scacz observed.

"Oh yes," I said fondly, patting the venting tubes that ran along its outer surface and collected the gases of the burning neem.

"How many do you think you can make?"

"At first?" I shrugged. "Perhaps it will take me a month to make another." The Mayor and Scacz both showed their consternation, and I rushed on. "But I can train other metal workers, other glassblowers. I need not do every piece of work. With others working to my specification. With a larger workshop, many more could be made."

"We could train the crafters who make the new arquebus," Scacz said. "Their work is obviously pointless. A weapon that can only be fired once and is so fussy, does not even pack the power of a decent crossbow and is slower still. But this?"

The mayor was nodding. "You're right. This is worth our effort. Those silly weapons are nothing to this."

Scacz took another sip of his wine, running his hand over the balanthast. A slow caress. "The potential here… is astonishing." He looked up at me, inquiring. "I think I would like to test it for a little while. See what it does."

"Majister?"

Scacz patted me on the back. "Don't worry. We'll be very careful with it. But I must examine it a while. Ensure that it truly uses no magic that will come back to haunt us." He looked at me significantly. "Too many solutions to bramble have simply sought to use magic in some glancing way. To build a fire, for example, and then when the bramble is burned, it turns out that so much magic was used in the making of the fire that the bramble returns twice as strong."

"But the balanthast doesn't use magic," I protested.

Scacz looked at me. "You are a majister to know this, then? In some cases, a man will think he is not using magical principles, because he is ignorant. You yourself acknowledge that something unique is afoot with this device." He picked up the balanthast. "It's just for a little while, alchemist. Just to be sure."

The Mayor was watching me closely. "Don't worry, alchemist. We will not slight your due reward. But for us, the stakes are very high. If we invest our office in something which brings the doom of Takaz instead of the salvation of Mara... I'm sure you understand."

I wracked my mind, trying to find a reason to deny them, but my voice failed me, and at that moment, Jiala started to cough again. I glanced over at her, worried. It had the deep sound of cutting knives.

Scacz began to gather up the device. "Go on," he said. "See to your daughter's health. She is obviously tired. We will send for you quite soon."

Jiala's coughing worsened. The two most powerful men in the city looked down at her. "Poor thing," the Mayor murmured. "She seems to have the wasting cough."

I rushed to contradict. "No. It's something else. The cold is all. It starts the cough and makes it difficult to stop."

Scacz pried the balanthast away from me. "Go then. Take your daughter home and warm her. We will send for you, soon."

⤙━✦━⤚

ALL THE way home, Jiala coughed. Deep wracking seizures that folded her small body in half. By the time we arrived at our doorstep, her coughing was incessant. Pila took one look at Jiala and glared at me with astonished anger.

"The poor girl's exhausted. What took you so long?"

I shook my head. "They liked the device. And then they wanted to talk. And then to toast. And then to talk some more."

"And you couldn't bring the poor girl back?"

"What was I supposed to do?" I asked. "'Thank you so much, Mayor and Majister, I must leave, and no, the lost wines of Jhandpara are of no interest to me. Name a price and I will sell you the plans for my balanthast, good day?'"

Jiala's coughing worsened. Pila shot me a dark look and ushered her down the hall. "Come into the workshop, child. I've already lit the fire."

I watched the two of them go, feeling helpless and frustrated. What should have been a triumph had become something else. I didn't like the way Scacz behaved at the end. Everything he said had been perfectly reasonable, and yet his manner somehow disturbed me. And the way the Mayor spoke. All his words were correct. More than correct. And yet they filled me with unease.

I made my way up the stairs to my rooms, empty now except for piles of blankets and a chest of my clothes.

Was I turning paranoid? Into some sort of madman who looked beneath everyone's meaning to some darker intention? I had known a woman, once, when I was younger, who had gone mad like that. A glassblower who made wondrous jewel pendants that glittered with their own inner fire, seeming to burn from within. A genius with light. And yet there was something in her head that made her suspicious. She had suspected her husband, and then her children of plotting against her, and had finally thrown herself in the river, escaping demons from the Three Hundred Thirty-Three Halls that only she could see.

Was I now filled with the same suspicions? Was I going down her path?

Mayor and Majister had both spoken with fair words. I unbuttoned my vest, astounded at how threadbare it had become. The red and blue stitching was old and out of mode. How broken it was. As was everything except the balanthast. It, at least, had gleamed. I had put so much hope into this idea, had spent so many years…

A knock sounded on my door.

"Yes?"

Pila leaned in. "It's Jiala. Her coughing won't stop. She needs you."

"Yes. Of course. I'll come soon."

Pila hesitated. "Now, I think. It's very bad. There is blood. If you don't use your spells soon, she will be broken."

I stopped in the act of fixing my buttons. A thrill of fear coursed through me. "You know?"

Pila gave me a tight smile. "I've lived with you too long not to guess."

She motioned me out. "Don't worry about your fancy clothes. Your daughter doesn't care how you dress."

She hurried me down the stairs and into the workroom. We found Jiala beside the fire, curled on the flagstones, wracked by coughing. Her body contorted as another spasm took her. Blood pooled on the floor, red as roses, brighter than rubies.

"Papa..." she whispered.

I turned to find Pila standing beside me with the spell-book of Majister Arun in her hands.

"You know all my secrets?" I asked.

Pila looked at me sadly. "Only the ones that matter." She handed me the rest of my spell ingredients and ran to close the shutters so no sign of our magic would be visible, reportable to the outside world.

I took the ingredients and mixed them and placed the paste on Jiala's brow, bared her bony chest. Her breathing was like a bellows, labored and loud, rich with blood and the sound of crackling leaves. My hands shook as I finished the preparations and took up Majister Arun's hand.

I spoke the words and magic flowed from me and into my child.

Slowly, her breathing eased. Her face lost its fevered glare. Her eyes became her own again, and the rattle and scrape of her breath smoothed as the bloody rents closed themselves.

Gone. As quickly and brutally as it had come, it was gone, leaving nothing but the sulphur stink of magic in the room.

Pila was staring at me, astonished. "I knew," she whispered. "But I had not seen."

I blotted Jiala's brow. "I'm sorry to have involved you."

Jiala's breathing continued to ease. Pila knelt beside me, watching over my daughter. She was resting now, exhausted from what her body had used up in its healing.

"You mustn't be caught, Papa." Jiala whispered.

"It won't be much longer," I told her. "In no time at all, we'll be using magic just like the ancients and we won't have to hide a thing."

"Will we have a floating castle?"

I smiled gently. "I don't see why not. First we'll push back the bramble. Then we'll have a floating castle, and maybe one day we'll even grow wines on the slopes of Mount Sena." I tousled her hair. "But now I want you to rest and sleep and let the magic do its work."

Jiala looked up at me with her mother's dark eyes. "Can I dream of cloud castles?"

"Only if you sleep," I said.

Jiala closed her eyes, and the last tension flowed from her little body. To Pila, I said, "Open the windows, but just a little. Let the magic out slowly so no one has a chance to smell and suspect. If you are caught here, you will face the Executioner's great axe with me."

Pila went and opened one of the windows and began to air the room, while I covered Jiala with blankets. We met again at the far side of the workshop.

At one time, I had had chairs in this room, for talk and for thought, but those were long gone. We sat on the floor, together.

"And now you are part of my little conspiracy," I said sadly.

Pila smiled gently. "I guessed a long time ago. She clearly has the wasting cough, but she never wastes. Most children, by this time, they are dead. And yet Jiala runs through the streets and comes home without a cough for weeks at a time. At least before she fell into bramble. The cough seemed to stay at bay unnaturally."

"Why did you not call the guards?" I asked. "There is a fine reward for people like me. You could have lived well by selling your knowledge of my foolishness."

"You don't use this magic selfishly."

"Still. It curses the city. The Mayor is right about that much. The help I visit upon Jiala, means that hurt is visited upon Khaim. Some neighbor of ours may find a bit of bramble growing in his flagstones. A potato woman in the field will till up a new bramble root, attracted by my healing spells. The bramble wall marches ever closer, and cares not at all what intentions I have when I use magic. It only cares that there is magic to feed upon." I stood stiffly and went to squat by the fireplace, rolled a log so that it crackled and set up sparks. Pila watched me, I could feel her eyes on me. I glanced back at her. "I help my child and curse my neighbor. Simple truth."

"And many of your neighbors do the same," Pila said. "Simple truth. Now come and sit."

I rejoined her, and we both watched the fire and my sleeping daughter. "I'm afraid I cannot save her," I said, finally. "It will take great magic to make the cough go away, entirely. Her death is written in the dome of the Judgment Hall, and I fear I cannot save her without great magic. Magic such as someone like Scacz wields. And he will not wield it for the sake of one little girl."

"And so you labor on the balanthast."

I shrugged. "If I can stop the bramble, then there's no reason not to use the great magics again. We can all be saved." I stared at the flames. Firewood had grown expensive since bramble started sprouting in the nearby forest. I grimaced. "We're caught in Halizak's Prison. Every move we make closes the walls down upon us."

"But the balanthast works," Pila reminded me. "You have found a solution."

I looked over at her. "I don't trust them."

"The Mayor?"

"Or the Majister. And now they have my balanthast. Another Halizakian box. I don't trust them, but they are the only ones who can save us."

Pila touched my shoulder. "I have watched you for more than fifteen years. You will discover a way."

I sighed. "When I add up the years, I feel sick. I was certain that I would have the balanthast perfected within a year or two. Within five. Within ten, for certain. In time to save Merali." I looked over at my sleeping daughter. "And now I can't help wondering if I'm too late to save even Jiala."

Pila smiled. "This time, I think you will succeed. I have never seen something like the balanthast. No one has. You have worked a miracle. What's one more, to save Jiala?"

She pushed her dark hair back, looking at me with her deep brown eyes. I started to answer, but lost my voice, struck suddenly by her proximity.

Pila...

With my work, I had never had time or moment to really look at her. Staring into her eyes, seeing the slight smile on her lips, I felt as if I was surfacing from some deep pool, suddenly breathing. Seeing Pila for the first time. Perhaps even seeing the world for the first time.

How long had I been gone? How long had I simply not paid attention to my growing daughter, or to Pila's care? In the firelight of the workshop, Pila was beautiful.

"Why did you stay?" I asked. "You could have gone on to other households. Could have made a family of your own.

I pay you less than when you did little other than washing and cleaning, and now you run the household entire. Why not move on? I wouldn't begrudge it. Other households would welcome you. I would recommend you."

"You want to be rid of me just as you reach success?" Pila asked.

"No—" I stumbled on my own words. "I don't mean to say…" I fumbled. "I mean, others all pay more."

She snorted. "A great deal more, considering that I haven't taken pay for more than a year."

I looked at her, puzzled. "What do you mean?"

She gave me a sad smile. "It was a necessary economy, if we were to keep eating."

"Then why on earth didn't you leave?"

"You wished me to leave?"

"No!" All my words seemed to be wrong. "I'm in your debt. I owe you the moon. But you starve here—you can't think that I do not appreciate. It's just that you make no sense—"

"You poor fool," Pila said. "You truly can't see further than the bell of your balanthast."

She leaned close, and her lips brushed mine.

When she straightened, her dark eyes were deep with promise and knowledge. "I chose my place long ago," she said. "I watched you with Merali. When she was well, and when she fell ill. And I have watched you with Jiala. I would never leave one like you, one who never abandons others, even when it would be easy. You, I know."

"All my secrets," I whispered.

"All the ones that matter."

5

THE NEXT DAY, THE Mayor again invited me to his great house on the hill, to demonstrate the mechanics of the balanthast.

Pila helped me with my finest once more, but now she leaned close, smiling as she did, our cheeks almost brushing, my mustaches quivering at the proximity of this woman who had suddenly come into view.

It was as if I had been peering through clouded glass, but now, had finally polished a clear lens. Our fingers met on the buttons of my vest and we laughed together, giddy with recognition, and Jiala watched us both, smiling a secret child's smile, the one that always touched her face when she thought she held some furtive bit of knowledge, but which showed as clearly on her expression as the fabled rocket blossoms of Jhandpara showed against the stars.

At the door, I hugged Jiala goodbye, then turned to Pila. I took a step toward her, then stopped, embarrassed at my forwardness, caught between past lives and new circumstance. Pila smiled at my uncertainty, then laughed and came to me, shaking her head. We embraced awkwardly. A new ritual. An acknowledgment that everything was different between us, and that new customs would write themselves over old habits.

I held Pila close and felt years falling away from me. And then Jiala crashed into us, hugging us both, together. Laughing and squeezing in between. Family. Finally, family again. After too long without. The Three Faces of Mara, all of us a little more whole, and grateful.

"I think she likes us this way," Pila murmured.

"Then never leave me."

"Never."

I left that empty house feeling more full of life than I had in years. Silly and full of laughter all at once. Thinking of weddings. Of Pila as a bride. A gift I had never hoped to find again. The weight of loneliness lifted from me. Even the bramble cutting crews didn't depress me. Men and women hacking bits of it from between the cobbles. Sweeping the city to make sure that vines didn't encroach. I smiled at them, instead. With the balanthast, people would at last be safe. Could at last live their lives as they saw fit.

In ancient Jhandpara, majisters imbued carpets with magic so that they could speed from place to place, arrowing across the skies. Great wide carpets, as big as a room, with silver tea services and glass smoking vessels all set out for their friends. Crossing the empire in the blink of an eye. Flying back and forth from their floating castles and their estates in the cool north, to their seasides in the gentle south. And children did not sicken and die, and there was no wasting cough. All things were possible, except that magic made bramble, and bramble dragged flying carpets from the sky.

But now I had the solution, and I had Pila's love, and I would have Jiala forever, or for at least as long any parent can hope for a child.

Not cursed at all. Blessed.

Out on the Sulong River, work was proceeding on the floating bridge. I couldn't help imagining what it would be like to have not just the one, but perhaps even three floating bridges. We could heat our homes in the winter with green magic flames. We could speed across the land. We could reclaim Jhandpara. I laughed in the sharp spring air. Anything was possible.

As I entered the Mayor's house, the steward greeted me with quick recognition, which put me more at ease. My fears of the night before had been erased by sleep and Pila's influence and the warming spring sunshine.

The steward ushered me into the audience gallery. I was surprised to find a number of notables also there, assembled in gold and finery: magistrates of the courts, clove merchants and diamond traders, generals and old nobility who traced their lineages back to Jhandpara. Even the three ancient Majisters of fallen Alacan. More people peered out from under the columned arches surrounding the gallery's marble and basalt flagstones. Much of Khaim's high and influential society, all gathered together.

I stopped, surprised.

"What's this?"

Majister Scacz strode toward me, smiling greeting. "We thought there should be a demonstration." He guided me over to a draped object in the center of the hall. From its shape, I guessed it was my balanthast.

"Is that my instrument?" I asked, concerned.

The Mayor joined us. "Of course it is. Don't be nervous, alchemist."

"It's a delicate device."

The Mayor nodded seriously. "And we have treated it with utmost respect." Scacz patted me on the back, trying to reassure me. "These people all around us are the ones whose support we need, if we are to effect your new balanthast workshop. We must raise taxes for the initial construction, and," he paused, delicately, "some of the old nobility may be interested in patronage, in return for ancient bramble lands reclaimed. I assure you, this is a very good thing. It's easier to gain support when people whiff profit than if they simply feel they are being taxed to no purpose." He motioned me to the balanthast. "Please, do not be nervous. All will be well. This is an opportunity for us all."

A servant brought in a huge pot, containing a cutting of bramble over seven feet tall. The thing seemed to fairly quiver in its pot, hunting malevolently for a new place to stretch its roots. They must have planted it the night before, immediately after I left, for it to have grown so large. Multiple branches sprouted from it, like great hairy tentacles.

The assembled dignitaries sucked in their breath at the sight of humanity's greatest enemy, sitting in the center of the gallery. In the light of day, with its hairy tendrils and milk-weed-like pods dangling, it spoke of eldritch menace. Even the pot was frightening, carved with the faces of Takaz, the Demon Prince, his serpent heads making offers of escape that would never be honored.

The Mayor held up his hands to the assembled. "Fear not! This is but a demonstration. Necessary for you to grasp the significance of the alchemist's achievement." He waved a hand at the servants and they lifted the drapery from my instrument.

"Behold!" the Mayor said to the throng. "The balanthast!"

The man had the gift of showmanship, I had to grant him that. The instrument had been polished, and now with sunlight pouring down from the upper galleries, it fairly blazed. Its glass chambers refracted the light, sending off rainbows. The copper bell mouths of its vents and the belly of its combustion chamber reflected the people in strange and distorted glory.

The crowd gasped in amazement.

"Has it been tampered with?" I asked.

"Of course not," Scacz said. "Just polished. That's all. I examined the workings of the thing, but took nothing apart." He paused, concerned. "Is it damaged?"

"No." But still I studied it. "And did it satisfy you? That it does not use magic? That it is not some device of the majisters pressed into new form?"

Scacz almost grinned at that. "I apologize most profusely for my suspicions, alchemist. It seems to function entirely according to natural properties. A feat, truly. History can only bow to your singular genius." He nodded at the assembled people. "And now, will you demonstrate for our esteemed visitors?"

As I began assembling the ingredients, a general in the audience asked, "What is this instrument of yours, Scacz?"

"Salvation, war lord."

A fat merchant, out of the diamond quarter with thick mustaches from his many children called, "And what is the use of it?"

The Mayor smiled. "If we told you, it would spoil the astonishing surprise. You must see it as the Majister and I first did. Without preface or preamble."

I armed the balanthast, but then had to have the servants help me drag it over until it stood beside the huge bramble pot. Under the assembled gaze, it seemed to take forever to scrape the tripod over the flagstones. Despite my faith in my device, my heart was pounding. I pulled on a leather glove and pinched out a bit of the potted soil. Added it to the firing chamber. Plunged the delivery nozzles into the dirt. At last, I lit the match.

For a moment, we all watched, silent. The collected ingredients burned, and then were sucked into the combustion chamber. A pause. I held my breath, thinking that Scacz and the Mayor had somehow broken the balanthast in their ignorance. Then the balanthast shook and the snake faces of the Demon Prince burst wide, spilling soil as the pot shattered. The bramble toppled and hit the marble. The crowd gasped.

Yellow smoke issued from the bramble's limbs. It writhed, smoking, twisting, boiling. Sap squealed and frothed as it effervesced, a dying howl from our ancient menace.

People covered their ears as the bramble thrashed. More smoke issued from its vines. Within a minute, the bramble lay still, leaving ash and tiny blackened threads floating in the sunlight. Yellow smoke billowed slowly over the assemblage, sending people coughing and wheezing, but as the clouds dispersed, a great murmuring rose at the sight of the scorched bramble corpse.

"Inspect it!" Scacz cried. "Come and see. You must see this to believe!"

Not many cared to come close, but the general did. Unafraid, he approached and knelt. He stared, thunderstruck. "There are no seeds." His wide-eyed gaze fell upon me. "There should be seeds."

His words carried through the crowds. No seeds. No seeds. The lightning strike of miracle.

The Mayor laughed, and servants arrived with goblets of wine for celebration. Scacz clapped me on the back and the men and women of the great merchant houses came to stare at the cleansed soil before them. And then Scacz called out again, "One further demonstration?"

The crowd clapped and stamped their feet. Again I primed the balanthast, eager to show off the wonder of our salvation. I looked around for another pot of bramble, but none was in evidence.

"How will I demonstrate?" I asked.

"It doesn't matter," Scacz said. "Let it ignite free."

I hesitated.

The Mayor said, "Don't be shy of a bit of showmanship. Let them see the glory."

"But it can't simply be fired. It must have something to attach to. Some bit of earth at least."

"Here." Scacz took something from his sleeve. "I have something else you might try this on." He said something under his breath and suddenly, I smelled magic. The scent was different from the healing magic I had cast upon Jiala the night before. This was something special. Bright as bluebells in the summer sun, sticky as honey. He pressed a folded bit of parchment into my palm.

"Put this in your balanthast chamber," Scacz said. "It should burn well."

The whiff of bluebell honey magic clung to the paper.

I didn't want to. Didn't know what he was up to. But the Mayor was nodding, and I was surrounded by the assembled people, all those great names and powerful houses watching, and the Mayor motioned me to continue.

"Go on, alchemist. Show us your genius. The crowd loves you. Let us see this thing fire free."

And to my everlasting regret, I did.

I braced the delivery nozzles so they poked into the air, and lit my match. The spelled parchment and the neem and all the assembled ingredients disappeared into the belly of the balanthast, and it roared.

Blue flame erupted from the nozzles, a long streak of sparkling fire. Thick yellow smoke issued with it. And something else: the sticky breath of the magic-laced parchment Scacz had given me. Flower brightness, volatilized in the belly chamber of the balanthast, and now released as smoke.

Beside me, Scacz's body began to glow an unearthly aura of blue, sharp and defined. But not just him. The Mayor as well. His steward also. I stared at my hands. Myself, even.

The fumes of the expended balanthast billowed through the room and others began to glow as well. The general. The fat diamond merchant. His wife. More women in their skirts. Men in their fine embroidered vests. But Scacz's blue-limned features were brightest of all.

"You were right," the Mayor murmured. "Look at us all."

Everyone was staring at the many people who now glowed with spirit fire, gasping at the wonder of their unearthly beauty.

Scacz smiled at me. "You were right, alchemist. Neem loves magic. It clings to its memory like a child to her mother's skirts."

"What have you done?" I asked.

"Done?" Scacz looked around, amused. "Why, just added a bit of illumination to your neem essence. Your fine alchemy and my simple spellcraft, combined. A lovely effect, don't you think?"

Boots thudded and steel rang around the hall. Guards appeared from behind white columns and beneath the arches. Men in scaly armor, and the tramp of more boots behind them.

"Seize them!" Scacz shouted. "All the ones who burn with magic's use. Every one! If they are not of the Mayor's office, they are traitors."

A babble of protest rose. Already the people who did not glow were shrinking from those that did.

The general drew his sword. "Treachery?" he asked. "This is why you bring us here?" A few others drew steel with him.

The Mayor said, "Sadly, war lord, even you are not immune to law. You have used magic, when it is expressly forbidden. If you have some excuse, the magistrate will hear you…" He paused. "Oh dear, it appears the magistrate is also guilty." He waved to his guards. "Take them all, then."

The general roared. He raised his sword and charged for the Mayor. Guards piled atop him like wolves. Steel clashed. A man fell back. The general stumbled from within the tangle of steel. Blood streamed from half a dozen sword thrusts. For a moment, I thought he would reach us, but then he fell, sprawling on the marble. And yet still he tried to reach the Mayor. Scrabbling like a beetle, leaving a maroon streak behind him.

The Mayor watched the general's struggle with distaste.

"On second thought, kill them all now. We know what they've been up to."

The guards howled and the blue-glowing nobility shrank before them. Too few were armed. They scattered, running like sheep, scrambling about the gallery as the guards hunted them down and silenced their begging. At last, there were no more screams.

I stood in the midst of a massacre, clutching my balanthast.

The Mayor waved to the guards. "Drag the bodies out. Then go and seize their properties." In a louder voice he announced, "For those of you still standing, the holdings of the traitors will be sold at auction, as is custom. Your trustworthiness is proven, and you shall benefit."

He clapped Scacz on the back. "Well done, Majister. Inspired, even." His eyes fell on my own blue-glowing form. "Well. This is a pity. It seems the Majister was right in all respects. He told me he smelled magic on you when we first met, and I didn't believe him. But here you are, glowing like a lamp."

I backed away, cradling the balanthast. "You're the Demon Prince himself."

"Don't be absurd. Takaz would care not at all for stopping bramble."

The guards were grabbing bodies and dragging them into piles, leaving blood smears behind.

The Mayor eyed the stains. "Get someone in here to mop these tiles! Don't just leave this blood here." He glanced around. "Where's my steward disappeared to?"

Scacz cleared his throat. "I'm afraid he was caught up in the general slaughter."

"Ah." The Mayor frowned. "Inconvenient." He returned his attention to me. "Well, then. Let's have the device." He held out his hands.

"I would never—"

"Give it here."

I stared at him, filled with horror at what he had done. What I had been complicit in. In a rush, I lifted the balanthast over my head.

"No!" Scacz lunged forward.

But it was too late. I threw down the balanthast. Glass vacuum chambers shattered. Diamond fragments skittered across marble. Delicate copper and brass workings bent and snapped. I grabbed the largest part of the balanthast, and flung it from me, sending it sliding, breaking apart into even smaller parts before coming to rest in the blood of its victims.

"You fool." Scacz grabbed me. His hand closed on my throat and he forced me down. The blue glow about him intensified, magic flowing. My throat began to close, pinched tight by Scacz's hate and power.

"Join the rest of the traitors," he said.

My throat bound shut. I couldn't breathe. I couldn't even cry out. No air passed my lips. The man was powerful. He didn't even need an inked page to spell such evil.

Darkness.

And then, abruptly, sunlight.

I could breathe. I lay on the flagstones and sucked air through my suddenly unbound throat. Majister Scacz knelt over me.

His hand lay upon my chest, resting gently. And yet, at the same time, I could feel each of his five fingers beneath my ribs. Gripping my heart. I batted weakly at his hand, trying to push him away. Scacz's fingers tightened, constraining the beat of my blood. I gave up.

I realized that the Mayor was standing over us both, watching.

"The Mayor points out that you are much too talented to waste," Scacz said. Again he squeezed my heart. "I do hope his faith proves true."

Abruptly his grip relaxed. He straightened and waved for the guards. "Take our friend to the dungeon, until we have a suitable workshop for him." His eyes went to the broken balanthast. "He has many hours of labor ahead."

I found my voice. Croaked out words. "No. Not this bloodbath. I won't be a part of it."

Scacz shrugged. "You already are. And of course you will."

6

HOULD I TELL YOU that I fought? That I didn't break? That I resisted torture and blandishment and took no part in the purge that followed? That I had no hand in the blood that gushed down Khaim's alleys and poured into the Sulong? Should I tell you that I was noble, while others pandered? That I was not party to the terror?

In truth, I refused once.

Then Scacz brought Jiala and Pila to visit. We all sat together in the chill of my cell, huddling under the water drip from stones, smelling the sweet damp rot of straw, and listening to the wet bellows of Jiala's lungs, the fourth participant in our stilted conversation.

Scacz himself said nothing at all. He simply let us sit together. He brought wooden stools, and had a guard provide cups of mint tea and at first I was relieved to see Jiala and Pila unharmed, but then Jiala's coughing started and wouldn't stop, and blood spackled her lips and she began to cry, and then I had to call the guard to take them away. And even though the man was fast in coming, it was still too slow.

The last vision I had of Jiala was of Pila carrying her small form, her wracking cough echoing against cold stones.

And then Scacz came down to visit me again. He leaned against the wall, studying my dishevelment through the bars.

"The cold of the dungeon disagrees with her lungs," he observed.

THE REPAIR of the first balanthast was the price of Jiala and Pila's well being, but Scacz and our Jolly Mayor were not finished with me. In Jiala they had the perfect lever. In return for the magic and healing that only Scacz could provide, I created the tools and instruments they desired. My devices purchased life for myself and my family, and death for everyone else.

Blood ran in the streets. Rumors in my prison said that the Mayor's halls were redder than a sunset. That bodies burned in bramble piles, the fat of their cooking twining with the yellow smoke of bramble to fill the skies with funeral pyres. The Executioner was so busy that on some days, a second and even a third were summoned to take over the efforts of the axeman who had grown exhausted with his work. Some days, they didn't even bother with the effort of a public spectacle.

Scacz had laughed at that.

"When we couldn't find these furtive little spell casters, we needed fear to keep the magic in check," he said. "Now that we can hunt them down, it's better to let them practice for a little while, and then seize everything."

As long as I furnished the tools of the hunt, I was not harmed. Scacz and the Mayor had so many uses for me. I was a prized hawk. Free enough, within certain confines. The dynamic between us was as taut as the strings on a violin. Each of us would pluck at those strings, seeking gain, testing the other's boundaries, trying the tenor of the note, the question of its strain. The workings of my mind and its creations tugging against the value of Jiala and Pila's well being. And so we each tugged and pulled at that catgut strand.

I was not a prisoner, precisely. More a scholar who worked all day and all night in a confined place, building better, more portable balanthasts. Constructing devices better tuned to sniffing out magic. Sometimes, I myself forgot my situation. When the work went well, I was as focused as I had ever been in my workshop.

I am ashamed to admit that there were even times when I reveled in the totality of focus that my cell provided. When there is nothing to do but work, a great deal of work can be done.

———※———

"COME NOW. I brought sweets. You like them," Pila urged. She sat outside the bars of my workshop, offering.

I sat, staring. "I'm not hungry anymore."

"I can see that. You're getting skinny."

"I was skinny before."

Pila watched me sadly. "Please. If you won't eat for yourself, then at least eat for me. For Jiala."

Unwillingly, I stood and shuffled over to her.

"You look unwell," she said.

I shrugged. Of late, I had been having nightmares. Oftentimes, I would dream of a river of my victims. Dreamed them pouring down the streets to where the Executioner stood waiting, the hooded butcher chopping off heads as they flowed past, his axe swinging like a scythe, heads spinning in all directions. And I stood at the source of that river, casting each person into the flow. Illuminating them in blue fire before tossing them into the current, sending them tumbling toward that final cataract of the axe.

Pila stretched her hand through the bars, and clasped my cold fingers. Her skin showed wrinkles and her palms showed surprising dryness. I thought that maybe those hands had been soft, that she had been young once, but I could hardly remember. She clasped my hand, and against all the promises I made myself, I collapsed against the bars, pressing her fingers to my cheek.

That I hungered for her warmth was something I could barely stand. Majister Scacz had offered us "relief" as he called it, but he did so with such a leer that after the first time, I could do it no more, and spat in his face when he next suggested the idea. Which enraged him so much that he barred Pila from visiting for nearly six months. Only when I threatened to cut my own throat with a bulb of glass did he finally relent and allow her visits again, if only through the bars. I kissed Pila's fingers, starved for her kindness and humanity in a place that I had turned brutish and bloody.

A few feet away, a guard sat, his body ostentatiously half-turned away from us, providing a semblance of privacy. This particular one was Jaiska. He had a family and his mustaches were long for his three sons, all of whom had followed him into the guards. Decent enough, and willing to give us a little privacy as we whispered to one another through the bars.

Not like Izaac, who loved to regale me with the executions he had seen, thanks to my inventions. Izaac said that within fifty miles of Khaim, no householder had passed untested by the balanthast. Heads not only decorated the city gates, but also the broad bridge that leaped the Sulong and now linked Khaim with its lesser kin. There were so many heads that the Mayor had gotten tired of mounting trophies and now simply ordered bodies tossed into the river to float to the sea.

"How is Jiala?" I asked.

"Better than you," Pila said. "She thrives. And grows. Scacz still refuses to let me bring her, but she is well. You can trust that. Scacz is evil but he loves your work and so he cares for us."

"Other people's heads in exchange for keeping our own." I stared at my workshop. "How many now have I killed? How much blood is on my hands?"

"It's no use thinking about. They were using magic, which was always forbidden. These are not guiltless people who go to the Executioner's axe."

"Don't forget that we were among them as well. Are among them, thanks to Scacz."

"There's no use thinking on it. It will only drive you mad."

I looked at her bitterly. "I've been here for two years already, and if I haven't found refuge in madness yet, I doubt I will."

She sighed. "In any case, it's slowing now. There are fewer who test the Mayor's powers of detection." She leaned close. "Some say that he now only finds magic on people who are too wealthy or powerful. Those ones he snuffs out, and confiscates their families and property."

"And no one fights?"

"A few. But he has supporters. The farmers near the bramble wall say the vines have slowed. In places, they even cut it back. For the first time in generations, they cut it back."

I scowled. "We could have cut back miles, if the Mayor had simply used the balanthast as it was intended."

"It's no use thinking on." She pushed a cloth-wrapped bundle of bread through the bars. "Here," she said. "Please. Eat a little."

But I shook my head and walked away from her offering. It was a petty thing. I knew it even as I did so. But there was no one else to lash out against. A petty rebellion for the real rebellion I had no stomach for.

Pila sighed. I heard a rustling and then her words to Jaiska. "Give these to him when he changes his mind. Some for you as well. Don't let him starve himself."

And then she was gone, leaving me with my workshop and my killing devices.

"Don't scorn her," Jaiska said. "She stands by you and your daughter when she could walk away easy. Old Scacz likes to bother her. Comes and bothers her."

I turned. "What do you mean?"

He shrugged. "Bothers her."

"She doesn't say so."

"Not to you. Wouldn't want you to do something stupid."

I sighed, feeling childish for my display. "I don't deserve her."

Jaiska laughed. "No one deserves anyone. You just win 'em and hope you can hang onto 'em." He offered me the bread. "Might as well eat while it's fresh."

I took the bread and cut a slice on a work table. Cut one for him as well. The scent of honey and rosemary, along with the reek of neem and mint and the burn of coals from my glass fire.

"It's a strange world we live in," I said, waving at my worktable. "All that time spent trying to find magic, and now, suddenly Scacz asks for balanthasts to kill bramble again. Maybe he'll finally decide to cut away the bramble wall."

Jaiska snorted. "Well. In a way." He took another bite of bread and spoke around the mouthful. "He cuts new lands into the bramble for his and the Mayor's friends. The people who inform for them. Their favored guards."

"Are you going to get new lands?"

Jaiska shrugged. "I'm just a sword. Keep my head down. Don't work magic when the hunters are out. Hope my sons all learn their sword swinging right. Don't need lands. Don't need honors. Don't do traffic with the Mayor."

I grimaced. "That's wisdom, there. I, on the other hand, thought I'd be a savior of our land."

"Bramble's mostly stopped." Jaiska said. "Hardly anyone except Scacz uses magic anymore. Not in any real way. Can't remember the last time I saw bramble sprouting in the city. We're saved. In a way."

"It isn't the way I hoped."

Jaiska laughed at that. "For being so clever with the devices, you're a damn silly-headed bastard."

"Pila said something similar to me, once."

"Because it's true, alchemist."

At the new voice, Jaiska leaped to his feet. "No offense, sir."

Scacz swept into view. "Go find something to do, guardsman."

"Grace." Jaiska touched his brow and fled.

Scacz sat down on the stool that Jaiska had vacated. His gaze came to rest on Pila's gift. "I'd ask you for some of that lovely bread, but I'm afraid you'd put bramble threads in it."

I shook my head. "Bramble threads would be too good for a creature like you."

"Ah. Yes. A creature. Indeed." He smiled. "A powerful creature, actually. Thanks to you. The most powerful majister in the land, now. The Majisters of Alacan all have their heads fitted to spikes." He sighed. "It really is an addiction. The feel of power flowing through... no one understands that. Siren song for those of us who have the knack. But then, you already knew that."

"I don't miss it," I said.

Scacz snorted. "Maybe. But the lure is certainly there. For many. For most. We could never allow the people to believe that your balanthast was actually a solution. False comfort there. As soon as they sipped a little magic from the pool, they would have demanded to drink deep. And then," he made a motion with his hands, "willy-nilly everyone would have been spelling here and there, charming and spelling and making flying carpets, and we'd all have a lovely time. Until the bramble overwhelmed us."

"It wouldn't have," I said. "We're not stupid."

Scacz laughed. "It's not as if the people of Jhandpara— of all the old empire—were unaware of magic's unfortunate effects. From the historical manuscripts, they tried mightily to hold back their base urges. But still they thirsted for magic. For the power, some. For the thrill. For the convenience. For the salvation. For the wonderful luxury."

He made a motion, and a castle appeared above his hand, glowing. It floated in clouds, with dragons of every color circling it.

"How could anyone give this up?" he asked. "The people of Jhandpara had no discipline. Even the ones who wished to control themselves lacked the necessary will. And so our Empire fell."

In Scacz's hand, the castle tumbled from its clouds, crashing into deep bramble forests below. Bramble spread over arched palaces, over coliseums, over temples to the Three Faces of Mara, growing tall and terrible. Dust and rubble clouds obscured the scene as more cloud castles fell.

Scacz brushed his hands together, obliterating the scene and knocking off a rain of dust that landed on his robes.

"Magic brings bramble," he said. "And even you, alchemist, hungered to use it."

"Only a little. To save my daughter."

"Every spell maker has a reasonable excuse. If we grant individual mercies, we commit collective suicide. A pretty puzzle for an ethical man like you."

"You think we're the same, then?"

"Magic is magic. Bramble is bramble. I couldn't care less what hairs a philosopher splits. Now, every night, I sleep knowing that bramble will no longer encroach. So I sleep very well indeed." He stood. Nodded at my new balanthast. "Hurry with your new device, alchemist. As always, your daughter's well-being depends upon it."

"Why not let me go?"

"Why would I do such a thing? Then you might go and carry this knowledge of balanthasts to some other city. Perhaps give others the illusion that discipline is no longer needed." He shook his head. "No. That would not do at all."

"Khaim is my home," I said. "I have no wish to leave. I could construct balanthasts. You say you want to cut back the bramble now. At last, our goals align."

"Our goals already align, alchemist." Scacz turned away. "Hurry with your tools. I have fiefs I wish to disburse."

"And if I refuse?"

Scacz turned back. "Then I simply will stop caring whether your daughter coughs up that river of blood of hers. The choice is yours. It always has been."

"You'll never let me go."

Scacz laughed. "I can't think why I would. You're far too useful."

THAT NIGHT I lay in my bed, surrounded by the weirdly comfortable smells and drips of my prison workshop, turning the problem of the Majister over in my head. I could not bargain with the dragon mind of Scacz. And despite his words, I suspected my time was running out.

Building balanthasts to create bramble fiefdoms was not the green grass of a new beginning, but the signal smoke of a bitter end. Once a brigade of balanthasts was prepared, there would be no more need of me.

I lay listening to the night guard's snores, and began to plan. Assembling pieces and components into a larger whole. Not a plan fully realized, but still… an intrigue. A tangle of misdirection, and at the end of its winding way, a path, perhaps, out of my Halizakian box. I considered the alleys and angles, testing chinks in the armor of my logic.

If I was honest, there were many.

But Pima, Jiala and I had already lived too long in the center of Khaim's bloody vortex. The storm would eventually tear us to pieces as well. Scacz might be a man of his word, but he was not a man of charity. The Mayor and Scacz thought in terms of trade, and when I had nothing left to offer, they would do away with me.

In the morning, I was up and constructing.

"Jaiska," I said. "Go find Scacz. Tell him I've had an inspiration."

When Scacz appeared, I made my proposal. "If you let me walk outside occasionally, I will make your detectors more powerful. I can extend their reach considerably, I think. And build them so that a man need not even handle them. They could run continuously, in market squares, all along the thoroughfares, at city gates."

Scacz looked at me suspiciously. "Why so amenable all of a sudden?"

"I want to live well. I want to see the sun and the sky, and I'm willing to bargain."

"You think to escape."

"From a great majister like you?" I shook my head. "I have no illusions. But I cannot live forever without fresh air." I held up an arm. "Look at me. I'm wasting away. Look how pale I become. Shackle me how you like, but I would breathe fresh air."

"How will you improve your design?"

"Here." I rolled out parchment and dipped my quill. Scratched out the bones of a design. "It would be a bit like a torch, standing. A sentry. It would issue a slow smoke from its boiler. Anyone who walked near would be caught." I pushed the rough sketch through the bars.

"You've been holding this back."

I met Scacz's gaze. "You should realize that keeping me alive and happy has benefits."

Scacz laughed at that, liking the bargain he thought we were making. "Does your hold on survival feel tenuous, alchemist?"

"I want assurances, Scacz. And a life. A life better than this."

"Oh? There's something else you desire?"

"I want Pila to be able to visit me again."

Scacz leered, then shook his head. "No. I think not."

"Then I will not improve your detectors."

"I could torture you."

I looked at him through the bars. "You have all the power, Majister. I ask for a favor and you return with threats. What else can I offer you? A better balanthast as well? Something that works faster and better than the ones you currently have? I can design ones that are light and portable. They could clear fields in days. Imagine the magics you could wield if bramble was hardly a threat at all."

And the hook was set. After all, what good is it to be the finest majister in the land when you cannot wield the finest, most impressive magics? Scacz's hunger to use his powers chafed against the natural limits that bramble imposed.

And so I set to work on my newly conceived balanthasts and my detectors. My workroom filled with supplies, with copper rolls, with bellows and tongs, with brass and nails, glass bulbs and vacuum tubes, and Scacz came to visit daily, eager for my promised improvements.

And Pila came to visit, as well.

In the darkness, we clutched close and I murmured in her ear.

"This cannot work," she whispered.

"If it does not, you must go without me," I said.

"I won't. It will do no good."

"Do you love Jiala?"

"Of course I do."

"Then you must trust me. Trust me as much as you did when I labored for so many years to get us into this mess."

"It's madness."

"A madness I created. And I must stop it. If I cannot, you must run. Take the spell for Jiala's health and go. Run as far as you can. For if I fail, Scacz will pursue you to the very ends of the earth."

In the morning, Pila left with a kiss and a copper token of my affection, bound around her wrist, a little bit of the workshop, leaving with her.

OVER THE course of weeks I worked, feverish. And at night, I met with Pila and whispered formulas and processes in her ear. She listened close, her long black hair tickling like feathers on my lips, the lustrous strands cloaking us as we played at intimacy and worked at salvation.

My detectors went up in the city, gouting out foul smoke and blanketing Khaim in their reactants, and once again blood ran in the streets. Scacz was well pleased. He granted me the privilege of letting me out of my cage.

I was so unfit that I ran out of breath simply walking up the stairs out of the dungeon. And then I gasped again when we reached the grounds and gazed over the city.

The flames of the detectors glowed here and there, blue fireflies sending out scented smoke that clung to anything magical at all. The bridge to Lesser Khaim blazed astonishingly bright, a beacon of magic in the thickening darkness.

"You have wrought something beautiful," Scacz said. "Khaim will always be known as the Blue City, now. And from now on, we will grow." He pointed into the sky, and I could see where the beginnings of a castle clung to wisps of accumulating clouds.

I sucked in my breath in astonishment.

"It's damnably difficult to summon and collect the clouds," Scacz said. "But it will be quite pretty when it's completed."

I felt as if I was staring at fabled Jhandpara. I could almost hear the music and taste the joy of the Mount Sena wine I had quaffed so long ago.

When I found my voice, I said, "You must bring the old balanthasts back to me so that I can adjust them. I will have to trade out their combustion chambers for the power that they will now wield."

Scacz smiled and rubbed his hands together. "And then I will truly be able to set to work on my castle. I won't have to check my powers at all."

"The Majister of the Blue City," I said.

"Indeed."

"I'd very much like to see it when it's done."

Scacz looked over at me, thoughtful. "If these balanthasts perform as you describe them, alchemist, then the very least I can do for you is to give you domicile above the earth."

"A prison in the air?"

"Better than one on the ground. You will have a most astonishing view."

I laughed at that. "I won't argue. In fact, I will hurry the moment." I turned to leave, but then paused, voicing an afterthought. "When the balanthasts arrive, I'll also need several pots of bramble. To test and make sure my designs are correct."

Scacz nodded, distracted, still staring up at the triumph of his castle. "What's that?"

"Bramble," I said patiently. "For the testing."

Scacz waved an acknowledgment, and the guards led me back down to my dungeon.

~~~~~

A FEW days later, I asked Jaiska to summon Scacz for the final demonstrations.

I had lined up a number of bramble plants in pots. "It would work better if we were at the bramble wall," I grumbled, "but this should suffice."

Along one wall, I had all the balanthasts of the city, lined up. Each one newly altered, its delivery tubes and chambers reshaped to their improved purpose. I took one of the gleaming instruments from its rank and plunged its nozzle into the bramble pot. The bramble's limbs quivered malevolently, as if it understood the evil I planned for it. The dry pods rattled as the pot shifted.

I lit the match, and pressed it into the new combustion chamber. Much faster and easier to ignite, now.

A low explosion. The plant thrashed briefly, and then disappeared in a puff of acrid smoke. There was simply nothing left of it at all.

I laughed, delighted.

"You see?"

Scacz and Jaiska stared, dumbfounded. I did it again, laughing, and now Scacz and Jaiska laughed as well.

"Well done, alchemist! Well done!"

"And it is prepared much more quickly now," I said. "These chambers on top mix the ingredients, so that they are always at the ready. Open this valve, and..." I lit another match. Explosion. Vented smoke. The potted bramble soaked up the balanthast's poison and disappeared in a squeal of burning sap and writhing smoke.

I grinned. Did it again and again, working something greater than magic in my workshop. Jaiska stamped his feet and whistled. Scacz's smile widened into a greedy astonished grin. And then I, laughing and in my folly, drunk on my success, grabbed a bramble with my bare hands.

A silly, reckless thing. A moment of inattention, and all my genius was destroyed.

I yanked my hands away as if the bramble was on fire, but its threadlike hairs clung already to my bare skin. The sleeping toxins numbed my hands, spreading like fire. I fell to my knees. Tried to stand. Stumbled and crashed into the balanthast, tumbling it and knocking it over, shattering it.

"Fool!" Scacz shouted.

I tried to get up once more, but fell back instead, tangling with bramble again. Its thorns pricked me, its threads clung to my skin, poisoning, clutching and hungry for me. Burrowing sleep into my heart, pressing down upon my lungs.

Darkness closed on my vision. It was terrifyingly fast. I crawled away, stupid with the toxins, reached through the bars. Scacz and Jaiska shied from my thread-covered hands.

"Please." I whispered. "Use your magic. Save me."

Scacz shook his head, staying well away from my touch. "No magic works against bramble's sleep."

"Please." I croaked. "Jiala. Please. Keep her well."

Scacz looked at me with contempt. "There's really no point, now, is there?"

My limbs turned to water. I slumped to the flagstones, still reaching through the bars as he went blurry and distant.

The Majister stared down at me with a bemused expression.

"It's probably better this way, alchemist. We would have had to chop your head off, eventually." He turned to Jaiska "As soon as he's done thrashing, gather up the balanthasts. And don't be so stupid as he was."

"What about his body? Should I take him to his wife?"

"No. Dump it in the river with the rest."

I was too far gone to panic. Bramble stilled my heart.

HAVING YOUR FLESH BURNED with blue flame is not my preferred method to awaken, but it is a great improvement over death. Another gust of flame washed over me. It burned through my blood, blistered my lungs, tunneled about in my heart, and dragged me back to life. I writhed in the heat, trying to breathe. Another blast of flame.

And suddenly, I was coughing and wheezing. My skin burned, but I breathed.

"Stop," I croaked, waving weakly for mercy, praying I wouldn't be scoured again. I opened my eyes.

Pila crouched over me, a fantastic jeweled balanthast in her hands. Jiala stood beside her, worried, clutching at her skirt.

"Are you alive, Papa?" she asked.

I pushed myself upright, shaking bramble threads from my arms. Pila looked me over, brushed me with a gloved hand. "He's alive enough, child. Now hurry and get our things. It's time for us to run."

Jiala nodded obediently and ran out of my workroom. I stared after her, astonished. How she had grown! Not a small child at all, but tall and vital. So much change in the two years I had been imprisoned. Pila continued to brush away the singed bramble thread. I winced at her touch.

"Don't complain," she said. "Blisters mean you're alive."

I flinched away from another round of brushing. "You found my body, it seems."

"It was a near thing. I was expecting a coffin to arrive. If Jaiska hadn't been decent enough to send word of where you'd been dumped…" she shrugged. "You were nearly tossed into the water with the rest of the corpses before I found you."

"Help me stand."

With her support, I made it to my feet. My old familiar workshop, but altered under Pila's influence.

"I had to replace much of the equipment," Pila explained as she braced me upright. "Even with your instruction, it was an uncertain thing."

"I'm alive, though." I looked at her balanthast. My design but her construction, noticing places where she had made changes. She held it by a leather strap that she slung over her shoulder. "You've made it quite portable," I said, admiring.

"If we're to run, it's time we did."

"More than time."

In the hall, our last belongings were stuffed into wicker baskets with harnesses to hold them upon our backs. A tiny pile of essentials. So little of my old life. A few wool blankets, food and water jugs. And yet, there also, Pila and Jiala. More than any man had any right to ask for. We slung our baskets, and I groaned at the weight in mine.

"Easy living," Pila commented. "Jiala could carry more than you."

"Not quite that bad, I hope. In any case, nothing that a long walk won't fix."

We ducked out into the streets, the three of us together, winding through the alleys. We ran as quickly as we could for the gates of Khaim, making our way toward the open fields. Inside, I felt laughter and relief bubbling up. My skin was burned, my hair was matted and melted, but I was alive, maybe for the first time in almost twenty years.

And then the wind shifted and a cloud of smoke blew across us. One of my own infernal detectors, now standing sentry on every street.

Jiala lit up like an oil lamp.

Pila sucked in her breath. "She was only treated yesterday. The magic still shows. Normally I kept her in, after Scacz spelled her."

Quick as a cat, she swept a cloak over Jiala, smothering the blue glow. And yet still it leaked out. Jiala's face shone an unearthly shade. I picked her up and buried her face in my chest. She was heavy.

"Don't show your skin, child."

We slunk through the city and out into the fields as darkness fell. We went along the muddy road, trying to hide my daughter's fatal hue. But it was useless. Farmers on the road saw and gasped and dashed away, and even as we hurried forward, we heard cries behind. People who sought to profit from turning in a user of magic.

"We aren't going to make it," Pila said.

"Run then!"

And we did, galloping and stumbling. I panted at the unaccustomed exercise. I was not meant to run. Not after years in prison. In a minute, I was gasping. In two, spots swam before my vision and I was staggering. And still we ran, now

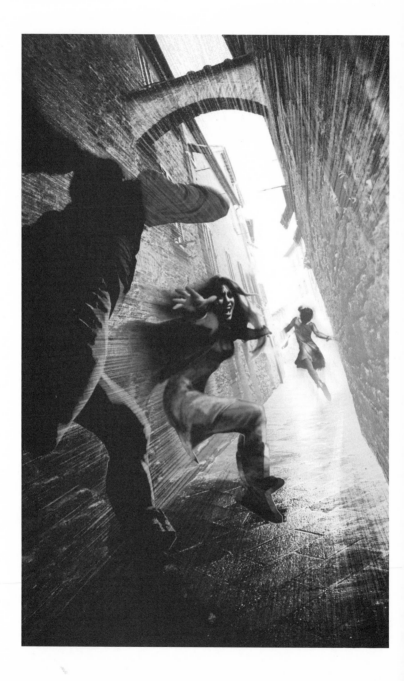

with Jiala on her own, tugging at me, dragging me forward. Healthier by far than I.

Behind us, the shouts of guardsmen echoed. They gained.

Ahead, black bramble shadows rose.

"Halt! In the name of Khaim and the Mayor!"

On the run, Pila fired her balanthast. Lit its prime. Prepared to plunge it into the ground at the bracken root.

"No!" I gasped. "Not like that." I lifted the device so it pointed into the guts of the bracken. "Don't hurt the roots. Just the branches."

Pila glanced at me, puzzled, then nodded sharply. The balanthast roared. Blue flame lanced from the nozzle, igniting the branches. Bramble writhed and vaporized, opening a deep narrow corridor of smoking writhing vines. We plunged into the gap. Another shout came from behind.

"Halt!"

An arrow thudded into a bramble branch. Another creased my ear. I grabbed Jiala and forced her low as Pila fired the balanthast again.

Behind us, the guardsmen were stumbling across the tilled fields, splashing through irrigated trenches. Their swords gleamed in the moonlight.

Blue flame speared the night again, and a writhing bramble path opened before us.

I pulled out the spell book of Majister Arun. "A match, daughter."

I struck the flame and handed it to Jiala. In its flickering unsteady light, I read spidering text by the hand of that long dead majister. A spell for sweeping.

A dust devil formed in the bracken, swirling. I waved my hand and sent it spinning down the narrow way behind us. A simple spell. A bit of household magic for a servant or a child. Nothing in comparison to the great works of Jhandpara.

But to the bramble all around, that tiny spell was like meat tossed before a tiger. The vines shivered at magic's scent and clutched after my sweeping whirlwind. I cast more small spells as Pila opened a way ahead. Bramble closed in behind, starving for the magic that I scattered like breadcrumbs, ravenous for the nurturing flavors of magic cast so close to its roots. Vines erupted from the earth, filling the path and locking us in the belly of the bramble forest.

Behind us, the guards' shouts faded and became indistinct. A few more arrows plunged into the bramble, ricocheting and clattering, but already the vines were thick and tangled behind us. We might as well have been behind a wall of oak.

Pila fired the balanthast again and we moved deeper into the malevolent forest.

"We won't have long before they follow us," she said.

I shook my head. "No. We have time. Scacz's balanthasts will not work. I crippled them all before I left, when Scacz thought I was improving them. Only the one I used for my demonstration worked, and I made sure to shatter it."

"Where are we going, Papa?" Jiala asked.

I pulled Jiala close as I whispered another spell of dust and tidying. The little whirlwind whisked its way into the darkness, baiting bramble, closing the path behind us. When I was done, I smiled at my daughter and touched her under her chin. "Have I ever told you of the copper mines of Kesh?"

"No, Papa."

"They are truly wondrous. Not a bit of bramble populates the land, no matter how much magic is used. An island in a sea of bramble."

The blue fire of Pila's balanthast again lit the night, sending bramble writhing away from us, opening a corridor of flight. I picked up Jiala, amazed at how heavy she had become in my years away, but unwilling to let her leave my side even for a moment, welcoming her truth and weight. We started down the corridor that Pila had opened.

Jiala gave a little cough and wiped her lips on her sleeve. "Truly?" she asked. "There is a place where you can use magic? Even for my cough?"

"As sure as balanthasts," I told her, and hugged her tight. "We only have to get there."

Another blast of blue flame lit the night, and we all forged onward.